THE ENTRE RÍOS TRILOGY

THE
ENTRE RÍOS
TRILOGY

Three Novels

PERLA SUEZ

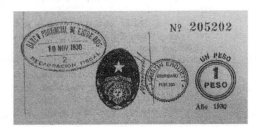

Translated by
RHONDA DAHL BUCHANAN

WHITE PINE PRESS | BUFFALO, NEW YORK

White Pine Press
P.O. Box 236
Buffalo, New York 14201
www.whitepine.org

This book was originally published in 2006
by the University of New Mexico Press.

Publication of this book was made possible, in part,
with funds from a Research and Creative Activity Grant
from the University of Louisville's
Department of Classical and Modern Languages.

Printed and bound in the United States of America.

Cover design: Elaine LaMattina

ISBN: 978-1-945680-59-5

Library of Congress number: 2022930232

*For my husband Bob. my first reader,
in deep appreciation for his loving support.*

CONTENTS

TRANSLATOR'S NOTE

In the Translator's Preface to the first edition of *The Entre Ríos Trilogy* (Albuquerque: University of New Mexico Press; Jewish Latin America Series, 2006), I referred to the process of translating the first three novels written by Perla Suez for adults as "a long journey" and "one of my most exhilarating adventures." Indeed, that exciting journey continued as I translated subsequent novels by the author: *Dreaming of the Delta* (Texas Tech University Press, 2014; *La pasajera*, 2008), *The Devil's Country* (White Pine Press, 2019; *El país del diablo*, 2015), *Red Smoke* (*Humo rojo*, 2012) and *Winter's Fury* (*Furia de invierno*, 2019). One of the most thrilling moments of this journey I shared with the author came in November of 2020, when it was announced that Perla Suez was the recipient of the XX Rómulo Gallegos International Novel Prize for her novel *El país del diablo*. The announcement of this coveted international prize, one of the most prestigious literary awards for an author who writes in Spanish, catapulted Perla Suez into the global limelight and sparked new interest in *The Entre Ríos Trilogy* and her other novels. After receiving messages from friends and strangers asking how they could purchase the English translation of the trilogy, I contacted the editors of the University of New Mexico Press to share the good news about the prize and the renewed interest it had generated for the trilogy. They informed me that the first edition of *The Entre Ríos Trilogy* was out of print and gave me authorization to find a new publisher for a second edition. I am very grateful to Dennis Maloney, the editor of White Pine Press, for taking on this project with such enthusiasm, after publishing *The Devil's Country* in 2019. The publication of this second edition of *The Entre Ríos Trilogy* was supported by a Research and Creative Activity Grant from the University of Louisville's Department of Classical and Modern Languages. I am indebted to Dr. Regina Roebuck, the Chair of my department, for her vision and support, and for making it possible for the trilogy to reach a much wider audience of English readers. I would also like to express my deepest appreciation to Perla Suez for her abiding friendship and constant encouragement.

This second edition includes the Translator's Preface that I wrote for the first edition, which details the journey that I embarked upon when I began translating the first novel of the trilogy in 2001. The original preface provides background information about Perla Suez and her ancestors, Ashkenazi Jews who escaped persecution under the rule of Czar Nicholas II and sought refuge in the agricultural colonies of Entre Ríos, Argentina, where thousands of immigrants settled at the end of the nineteenth century. It was in the town of Basavilbaso, Entre Ríos, that Perla Suez spent the first fifteen years of her life and absorbed family stories handed down by her grandparents and parents, tales that later would make their way into the stories she would write for children and novels for adults. Since the publication in 2006 of the *Trilogía de Entre Ríos* in Spanish and its translation to English that same year, Perla Suez has ventured beyond the confines of her childhood province into other regions of the country to explore the role that violence and authoritarianism have played throughout Argentina's history. Whether Suez sets the action of her novels in the provinces of Entre Ríos, the Chaco, Patagonia, or the territories bordering Paraguay, Brazil, and Argentina, readers will perceive in her characters the basic weaknesses of human nature that may lead to destruction, as well as the triumph of the human spirit in overcoming social injustice.

—Rhonda Dahl Buchanan

TRANSLATOR'S PREFACE

The journey, in its myriad forms, appears as the leitmotif in the narrative fiction of Perla Suez, whose characters travel by boat, train, car, trolley, surrey, horse, and foot, and by flights of memory that often evoke the harsh realities of Jewish persecution in the Old World and anti-Semitism in their adopted homeland of Argentina. Suez's characters retrace the steps that brought her ancestors from Odessa and Besarabia in Eastern Europe to San Gregorio, Villa Clara, and Basavilbaso, the Jewish agricultural colonies of the Entre Ríos province, where the author spent the first fifteen years of her life. As a young girl growing up in the town of Basavilbaso, Suez absorbed family stories handed down by her grandparents and parents, such as the terrifying account of how her paternal great-grandparents were murdered by Cossacks in a pogrom during the reign of Czar Nicholas II. Years later, the author would incorporate aspects of those tales of adventure, passion, and violence into her short stories for children and novels for adults.

In June of 2000, Suez sent me her first novel written for adults, *Letargo*, which had just been published by the Editorial Norma in Buenos Aires. Little did I know when I read the novel for the first time that I myself was about to embark on a long journey. A year later, in June of 2001, I began to translate *Letargo*, and in doing so, immersed myself in a world that I could only experience from an outsider's perspective, for I am neither Jewish nor Argentine. In July of 2003, I traveled to Entre Ríos with the author and her husband, Roberto Suez, to visit the land of her great-grandparents and grandparents, the fictionalized world of *The Entre Ríos Trilogy.* The author gave me a guided tour of her childhood home in Basavilbaso, which serves as the model for the protagonist's house in *Lethargy.* Later that day, we visited the cemetery of San Gregorio and placed stones on the tomb of her grandmother, an ancient Jewish tradition that serves as a token of remembrance. In Concordia, we saw the rice fields which are so integral to the novel *The Arrest,* and in Pueblo Liebig, a town founded by the British in the early twentieth century, we visited the meatpacking plant along the Uruguay River, which is featured in the third novel, *Complot*.

Although I have spent nearly twenty years of my academic career studying the fascinating history and culture of Argentina and have visited the country on many occasions, the process of translating this trilogy of novels has been one of my most exhilarating adventures. Umberto Eco writes in *Experiences in Translation* that "every language expresses a different world-view" and "translation is always a shift, not between two languages but between two cultures."(Toronto: University of Toronto Press, 2001, p. 17.) Indeed, as I crossed the borders back and forth from source to target language, I found myself faced with the challenge of finding the appropriate words and style to capture the unique "world-view" that Suez offers her readers.

For Perla Suez, writing is a journey in which memory and dreams play a crucial role. The past infiltrates and informs the present in her novels, and readers may notice that the narration often shifts from the present to the past, and from first person to third person within the same paragraph. Wide spaces between paragraphs and the use of ellipsis mark these temporal and spacial shifts, and also suggest that in this fictitious world, secrecy and silence conceal the truth, and often what is not said is as significant as what is spoken.

Aside from the physical journey that I made to Argentina while translating these novels, I also made a virtual voyage, researching the historical events and processes that Suez intertwines in her narrative fiction, beginning with the immigration of Jews from Russia to Argentina in the late nineteenth century, followed by the rise of leftist unions and anarchist movements during the early decades of the twentieth century. *The Arrest* is set against the historical events that occurred in Buenos Aires during *La Semana Trágica*, the "Tragic Week" in January 1919 when government forces, in the name of order and patriotism, arrested, tortured, and murdered striking workers and many innocent people, particularly those of Jewish descent. *Complot* chronicles the vast influence of Great Britain in the building of the

Argentine nation during the early twentieth century, through land investment, development of the railway system, cattle ranching and exportation of meat products, prostitution, and other corrupt business ventures. The stifling atmosphere of intolerance, paranoia, and repression during the 1950s is captured in *Lethargy*, and as is the case in the other two novels, the narration of past events prefigures the most violent period in Argentine history, which took place during the dictatorship of 1976 to 1983.

The most exciting and rewarding part of traveling is the pleasure and the privilege of sharing the experience with others. Many people accompanied me on this journey, and I would like to thank them for "sharing the ride." To begin with, I would like to thank my friend, Perla Suez, for her invaluable assistance and support in the preparation of this translation, and for her trust in me to provide readers of English with an authentic glimpse into her imaginary universe. Indeed, it was a leap of faith for the author to place the translation of these novels in my hands because until recently, she did not speak English, except for the expression, "I am a backseat driver," which I taught her during our trip to Entre Ríos. At times it was a challenge for this "city slicker" to find the exact name in English for the many birds, insects, flowers, plants, trees, fish, and animals that are native to the province of Entre Ríos. They say a picture is worth a thousand words, and I am indebted to Larry Page and Sergey Brin, the two genuises who created Google, for the internet sites that helped with this research. Using their internet search engine, I consulted hundreds of websites in my quest for the most authentic words to translate Perla's visions. Images flew from Louisville, Kentucky, to Córdoba, Argentina, via email for the author to confirm my discoveries, and this method, along with numerous email explanations, proved to be the most efficient way of identifying the many wonders that populate the fictional landscape of *The Entre Ríos Trilogy*.

Over the past few years, I have been fortunate to be able to consult experts to help me select the appropriate vocabulary for passages concerning activities beyond the scope of my knowledge and experience. I woud like to thank the Argentine writer Ana María Shua, who provided explanations of certain Jewish customs that appear in *Lethargy*, and her husband, Silvio Fabrykant, who helped with terminology regarding the art of photography in the same novel. Many thanks to Alberto Livore and Raúl Schinder, two "cultured" rice farmers from the city of Concordia, Entre Ríos, who taught me lessons about the delicate trade of rice cultivation, which figures prominently in *The Arrest*. I would like to thank another Argentine writer and mutual friend of Perla Suez, Tununa Mercado, who visited Louisville in September of 2004 and earned her room and board at the "Buchanan Bed & Breakfast" by deciphering the *lunfardo* expressions in the lyrics of an old tango that appears in *The Arrest*. Mercado, who is as renowned for her cooking as she is for her fiction, also identified the many animal parts shipped from the meatpacking plant in La Lucera to London in *Complot*. I did not have to look far to find an expert to help me with the duck hunting and fishing scenes found in the third novel. I would like to express very special thanks to my father, Ronald Lee Dahl, who has spent nearly seventy years hunting in the hills of western Pennsylvania, where he grew up, and fishing on the shores of the Chesapeake Bay, where he has lived for the past thirty years.

I am a firm believer that two heads are better than one, so I invited many people to read the manuscripts of one, two, or all three novels of the trilogy, and I would like to express my appreciation to all of them. First and foremost, I am grateful to my husband, Bob Buchanan, who not only was the first person to read all three novels and give me excellent suggestions, but also offered encouragement and support throughout the long process of tranlating this book. I would like to thank Guillermo Astigarraga, Tamar Hellar, David William Foster, and Dianna Niebylski for their insightful comments on *Lethargy* during the very early stages of this translation project. I am very fortunate to work with two professors of Spanish with expertise in translating: Clare Sullivan and Mary Makris. My deepest apprciation to both of them for their valuable assistance, and also to Lucy O'Farrill, Sylvia Berger, Mara Maldonado, and Mary Beth Regan for their editorial advice. I would also like to thank my colleagues in the Department of Classical and Modern Languages, who verified the accuracy of expressions in Russian, Yiddish, French, Italian, German, Portuguese, and Latin that appear in the novels.

In the summer of 2004, I was selected to participate in a residency program at the Banff International Literary Translation Centre in Banff, Canada, where I had the opportunity to consult with Margaret Sayers Peden about the trilogy. I would like to thank the Banff Centre for the translation award, Petch Peden for her advice, and Cristina de la Torre, one of my fellow Banff "Terrific Translators," for her careful reading of *Lethargy*. I would also like to acknowledge support from the University of Louisville for the Richard and Constance Lewis Fellowship, which financed my trip to Argentina in 2003, and the 2004 Intramural Research Incentive Grant, which enabled me to complete this project.

Last, but certainly not least, I would like to express my sincere gratitude to Ilan Stavans for inviting me to participate in the Jewish Latin American Series, which he edits for the University of New Mexico Press. After reading my translation of the first novel, he suggested that I translate the second and third novels in the trilogy, even before the author had finished writing *Complot*, and I thank him very much for his confidence in me. Finally, I would like to thank David Holtby, Senior Editor of the University of New Mexico Press, and his editorial assistant, Sonia Dickey, for making this dream that I share with Perla Suez a reality that will be shared now with many others.

—Rhonda Dahl Buchanan

LETHARGY

FOR ROBERTO

. . . I only want to ask you for one thing, something
that costs nothing: the story of your life . . .
—*Giovanni Papini*

Lete: one of the slow-moving rivers of Averno,
along whose shores wandered souls,
forced to drink from her waters,
which made them forget the past.
—*from Greek mythology*

JOURNAL 1

A stir of distant voices rises dimly: two women argue in the middle of the street, and I can't make out what they're saying. I'm on the sidewalk, standing on one foot on the number three that I just drew with a piece of brick. It must be Friday, because I see Bobe at the very moment she covers her head with a handkerchief, and her eyes with her hands, to recite the prayer over the candles.

Papa, who doesn't believe in God, fixes the latch on the living room window, and Mama knits a light-blue blanket, while I watch how she wraps the yarn around the needle, her fingers moving on their own, and her eyes on us.

The light is faint, and the raindrops tap against the metal awning over the patio. The rain's getting into the house. There's a leak in my room, and the water falls at the foot of my bed. I hear Bobe setting pots everywhere.

Later, Bobe shows me how to embroider and emboss silk on a frame.

The girl holds her breath when she thinks about her father, when she imagines him sinking once more into the wicker chair, his long legs intertwined, waiting for her mother to tell him, "Merke, dinner's getting cold." The girl sees her mother sitting at the table, sighing over her swollen belly. Her mother counts the knives and forks, and when Bobe asks why she counts them, she says she does not know.

We eat after my grandmother closes the shop. Bobe doesn't speak, and Papa tucks the napkin under his chin, dunks a piece of bread in the gefilte fish broth, and doesn't say a word either. Mama looks at me as if through a frosted pane of glass.

The house is immersed in silence, and the silence deepens whenever the wind stops beating the window, and the girl, with her nose pressed against the glass, hears the drumming of raindrops on the patio awning.

When I walked in that morning, Bobe had everything cleaned up and the table set.

"Lete's water broke," I heard Papa say, as he rubbed his hands on his legs, not knowing what to do.

Papa was tall and thin, and had to bend over to pass through the doorway. He had sad eyes, and never knew what to do with his hands, if he didn't have them in the pockets of his jacket. He hovered over Bobe until she said, "Stop following me, Merke."

For the first time, I ate breakfast without Bobe filling my bowl. She spoke to Papa in Yiddish in a long, anxious whisper, and then said to me in a nervous tone I'd never heard before, "I don't want you to go near your mother's room."

"She'll just go in for a minute," Papa said.

"No, you won't. Your mother shouldn't get excited."

Then she added with a sigh, "The stork will come through the transom."

Papa whispered in my ear that I shouldn't get Bobe more upset than she already was. I left the house and wandered aimlessly for an hour or more. I crossed the train tracks and went through the turnstile, when suddenly, a man appeared wearing a raincoat. I could see his face, and then I saw Leibe's calf, and I watched the man who had bought it put the calf in his truck and drive off, kicking up a cloud of dust.

I walked into the kitchen and overheard Bobe telling Papa that you need money to bring children into the world. And I heard Papa swear, "*Kishen tukhes.*"

And he stood there like a shadow by the living room window, with a cigarette in his mouth. I can barely make out his face, with its three-day-old beard, and yet, I'm sure that Papa is Papa, and he's standing there, motionless, on that dreary day, by the window, staring into the emptiness. It's dark outside, and until it clears, I'll be the girl who walks in the mist.

I'm picking up some of Bobe's habits. She doesn't spend because she wants to be sure she has money, and that it's in a safe place, somewhere only she knows. The day I went with her to Frenkel's store, she haggled over the price of a saltshaker, and because she couldn't get it for less, she left the store complaining about the bad service, telling me the saltshaker she'd picked out was the lousiest one she'd ever seen. Naturally, in her shop everything had a fixed price, and when someone, like Aunt Berta, asked for a discount, she'd say with a painful look on her face, "It's not that I don't want to, my dear, it's that I can't."

And Bobe would tell Aunt Berta the story of Mama's wedding again, saying how sorry she was that Aunt Berta hadn't attended the wedding, just to make her sigh. She'd describe in detail the lace dress Mama wore that night, and would only interrupt the conversation to offer Aunt Berta a cup of tea. Bobe would get her all wrapped up in her tale. At times, she'd be gracious, and tell her that God would reward her for caring for Mama the way she did, and Aunt Berta would listen to her, pleased. In Bobe's story, Mama was a queen, and when she told Aunt Berta that Mama fell in love with Papa the very first time she laid eyes on him, Bobe seemed lost in an intense dream, and Aunt Berta would sigh.

The truth is, things weren't as Bobe wished, but it was a matter of saving face to say her daughter had married well, and she'd make things up so that Aunt Berta would stay and listen to her.

The girl is still there, deep inside her, although now she does not remember everything she wants to recall. For that to happen, she will have to return to each image, each taste, each sensation of touch, to the smallest memories embedded in her flesh.

Mama was in her bathrobe, leaning over me, and I was ready to go to sleep, but first I wanted her to tell me again how the ugly duckling got lost. So Mama repeated once more the story of the duck who looked for his mother everywhere, and she stressed that none of the other animals would take pity on the ugly duckling. And I remember holding Mama's hand, and trying not to fall asleep until the duck returned to his house at the edge of the forest, where his mother was waiting for him.

Papa asks me if I want a brother or sister, and I tell him I don't know. Bobe tells Papa to hurry and get Sheine Malke.

The girl can still hear her grandmother saying, "Don't go out in those pants, you hear me?"

The girl asks her father if she can go with him, but he says no. And she watches him through the window, and when she sees him drive the station wagon over the railroad crossing, she thinks she hears the jingle of the signalman's bell.

As she puts on her shoes, she thinks about her mother. When she asks Bobe again to let her go in, her grandmother responds, "Did you eat the *knishes* I left for you?"

The girl does not answer, and her grandmother grabs her by the arm. "Go to your room."

I shut myself up in my room, and looked out the window and was happy I'd thrown the knishes to the geese. The afternoon slipped by and it started to rain. I don't know how long I stayed there, gazing at the deserted street. I don't know how long that girl was at the window, standing still, watching the rain fall silently to the ground.

I heard Bobe walking around the shop. And the girl also heard the noise of the metal blind being lowered, and when the door opened, she saw her grandmother crush her with a glare.

She had never felt like that before, the way she did on the afternoon her brother was born. It was cold, and something in her stomach kept her from breathing. That was her room: the brass bed, the mirrored wardrobe, and on a chair, the rag doll her mother had made for her.

Bobe returns and says she can go to León's house. The girl hears her mother moan, and imagines her lying in a pool of blood.

Papa walked in looking pale, wrapped in his shawl, and said that Sheine Malke was delivering another baby, but would come later. Then he said they should take Mama to the hospital. Bobe said they should wait for Sheine Malke, adding, "And if she doesn't come, I'll handle it myself."

The girl watches her grandmother wash her hands, tear a sheet into strips, run scissors through the flame on the stove, and carry a bowl of water into the room, silent and determined. She is not interested in her brother; she only sees her mother lying in a pool of blood.

Mama screamed, "Sheine Malke, help me!"

"Bring another towel, Merke!" Bobe ordered.

And I thought Mama was going to die.

The chandelier is covered with tulle because Bobe says the flies dirty the crystals. At one moment, before my brother is born, I hear Papa and Bobe speaking in Yiddish, and I wonder if what they're saying has to do not only with something I don't know, but also with something I shouldn't know.

Bobe told me not to take my eyes off the transom. And I can see myself, upset over the thought of a bird with a long beak coming from the sea, bringing my brother. And I see myself bending over Leibe, pulling the feet of her calf as it strains to come out of the bleeding hole between the cow's hind legs.

The girl sleeps, hugging her rag doll, and dreams that someone is telling her to hurry. Suddenly, she hears a scream, and then Bobe shouting, "It's a boy!"

My brother's cries ring in my ears endlessly. I ran without stopping in the rain, down the street to the cornfield, where I hid among the sharp stalks. Perhaps I fell asleep.

I headed back home and stopped at a corner, sinking my feet into the soft mud. A bolt of lightning lit up the street, and the floodlight on the lamppost danced in the wind.

The girl walks into the house, and she sees her mother, and is no longer afraid she will die. She sees her mother's breasts are swollen, and hears her say they hurt.

Mama opens the drawer of the nightstand, and takes out a pill, and I give her a glass of water and say, "Just take half."

"I like it when you take care of me," she says, with a pale, distant shimmer in her light violet eyes.

Her stare is so intense, I finally look away. Now she walks around the room while my brother sleeps. Papa isn't with her. I bring her tea, and put two lumps of sugar in the cup, and she smiles.

Later, Papa comes in from Bobe's shop, which is separated from the house by a door, and I hear him say to Mama, raising his voice, "Doctor Yarcho will perform the circumcision in the hospital."

"If the rabbi doesn't do it, he'll always be a *goy*," Bobe replies.

"I wasn't talking to you!" Papa retorts.

Then Mama cries out that she has a splitting headache.

"It's all right, Lete, it's all right," Papa tells her.

And her father goes out to the patio, and the girl follows him. He says he wants to be alone, but she does not leave his side. She strokes his hands, and he lets her caress them, even though he is trembling. Later, when heavy raindrops pound the patio awning, he says they should go inside.

The *bris* was performed as Bobe wished.

The girl slips in and out of the crowd, and hears her brother crying. When she moves closer, she hears the sound of metal hitting the bucket: everything is over. Her father has tears in his eyes, and while everyone celebrates, the girl thinks how lucky she is to have been born a female, even though she remains silent when she wants to speak, and listens to what a girl should not hear.

JOURNAL 2

The girl sees that her mother has tears in her eyes while her son suckles her nipple.

"Why don't you stop nursing him?" Papa tells her.

Then Bobe intervenes, with her face all flushed. "Who are you to tell a mother how to care for her child?"

The girl sees her mother sitting there in the living room, amid the furniture she remembers so well, staring intently at a sheet of stationery. The girl asks her whom she is going to write, and her mother looks up, but does not answer. The light is blinding, and reaches farther than the eye can see.

Later, I hear Mama say that she has a lump in her throat, and Papa repeat that he doesn't like to see her that way. His voice trembles when he says, "Remember what I told you, cows' milk will make him strong."

That night, the girl dreams that she is walking through silent corridors, and comes to a white square, where she sees her parents. The sun is out and it is foggy. The girl watches her mother cover her brother's carriage with a nearly invisible net, and she hears the baby crying inside. She screams that the net is a spider web, and shouts for them to take it off, but her mother just laughs with glee.

When I woke up, I heard Papa mumbling, "Now I know I'm not worth a thing to your mother."

And I heard Mama crying and saying, "Enough, enough . . ."

What happened next still goes on inside me.

Her father keeps the books for her grandmother's shop, and often stays up late into the night. It was hard for Bobe to find fault with him because Papa was meticulous. Bobe made it her business to know what time he came home.

Papa liked politics. It was the only thing he really enjoyed. Whenever he had a meeting, he'd leave the shop early. That would irritate Bobe, and she'd ask, "Are you going out again?"

The girl follows her father. He stops, looks at her intently, and gently tells her to go back. She is a girl who is no longer a child, and yet she clings to him, holding him back by his arm. He says something and leaves. As he walks away, she does not even listen to her father's footsteps on the sidewalk. Her face vanishes in the pale light.

The girl looks out the window into the darkness, and listens to the fury of the wind banging the shutters.

Her father returns and sits down by his wife. He tells her in a whisper that he has joined the Party. Without looking at him, she asks if he has thought it through. Her father lights a cigarette and says that everything is so unfair. And then he goes on about the evil in the world, blaming private property for all the bad things in life. And he talks about Marx and Lenin.

Bobe is always listening.

The girl shivers when Bobe tells her father that she is not going to allow a Communist to work for her, and when he replies that he considers himself fired.

As her father leaves, he says to the girl, "Honey, let's go out and get some ice cream."

"Why does Bobe say you're strange?"

Her father smiles at her, but does not answer, and she whispers, "Papa, I don't want the two of you to fight."

He lifts her up with his thin arms.

"My girl," he says, and kisses her cheeks.

Papa got a job at the Bank of Entre Ríos, and Bobe hired a bookkeeper. Mama only went into the shop to look for a remnant, or to thank a customer for bringing her vegetables and eggs.

Bobe worried that someone might call her son-in-law a Communist. She'd lived through the Czar's regime, the terrors of the pogrom, and was a woman who feared only God; however, according to what Papa used to say, she talked as if she were rich. The very same Bobe who never had two coins to rub together.

Aunt Berta was the best friend Mama had. She was the only friend from school Mama hadn't forgotten. They were separated when Aunt Berta moved with her family to Nogoyá, but got in touch again before my brother was born, and ever since then, Aunt Berta would always come to the house and drink *mate* with Mama, while they reminisced about their school days.

One morning, Aunt Berta told Bobe she thought Mama seemed sad. Bobe said not to make so much of it, and when Aunt Berta left, she went into the kitchen and started chopping an onion frantically. Bobe said to me, spitting out her words, "Besides being a fat, ugly spinster, that woman's also a Communist."

One afternoon, Papa came home early from the bank, and Mama begged him, "Merke, take me to the Astral."

"What's playing?" he asked.

"*An Affair to Remember.*"

When they came home, Mama grumbled that Papa had fallen asleep in his seat.

Sometimes her mother has to settle for a walk around the block, saying, "At least I can get some fresh air." Other times she goes with Aunt Berta to the square, and they take the girl with them. There is a wall at one end that she likes to walk across, like an acrobat on a tightrope.

On Sundays, they would take Bobe to the cemetery. One morning, after they left, León invited me to go hunting for partridges. His parents weren't home, and he loaded his father's shotgun with pellets, and we went into the fields.

The girl tells León she sees a partridge, and runs just as he takes a shot. The pellet wounds her left knee. At that moment, she thinks she is going to die.

A man in a truck who happens to be driving by takes her to the nearest hospital. The doctor bandages her, without taking his eyes off her, and says the buckshot barely grazed her knee.

Of all the things I found in the house where I grew up, there's something I can't forget: the letter that an uncle of Bobe's wrote her. The uncle lived in Buenos Aires. It was written in Yiddish, and the words ran together from right to left, from east to west, like a murmuring stream of ink that Bobe would read out loud, with undeniable pleasure.

One afternoon, an adult León said to me, "Why don't you do something with all that?"

I remember Bobe reading her uncle's letter, where I'm sitting now, and I tremble, as if it were happening today. Those letters ripple once again over the sheet of paper, which I hold in my hands, as if they were an army, spreading out over the white paper, as far as the eye can see. As if they were the soldiers of Aleksandr Kerenski, there, on the horizon.

The sound of footsteps coming and going woke me, followed by screams.

I heard Doctor Yarcho saying that my brother had died in his sleep.

"Crib death," he said.

Papa also said, "Crib death," with a raspy, broken voice. My brother was in his cradle. They'd covered him up, but Bobe uncovered his face so that I could say goodbye. It was the first time I'd ever seen someone dead. I looked at Papa, and I looked at Mama, who seemed lost. And I looked at Bobe, who cried out over and over, "*Mein kind*, with those rosy cheeks."

I couldn't forget how my brother used to suckle Mama's breast, and search anxiously for her nipple whenever he let go of it. I tell myself my brother's death could have happened yesterday. I tell myself his death can still happen now.

The town was covered in mist as we left, and the road was black and muddy. When we returned home, I looked at my room, and it wasn't the same. That night, and many other nights, I dreamed my brother was stretching his arms out for me to pick him up.

The girl hears her mother say that her vision gets blurry, and that if she tries to stand up, she feels dizzy.

I tell her, "Mama, it's five o'clock in the afternoon," and I wake her up. I help her to the armchair, although she prefers the bed.

She won't let us open the shutters. She says, "Just the lamp on the nightstand," and also says she prefers to be in the dark. I sit by her side. Mama takes in everything around her, and then looks at me.

The fragrance of rose marmalade rises as her mother dunks the petals into the syrup. The perfume enters the girl, and goes down her throat, until it is buried deep inside her body.

It's strange, but this morning when I was thinking about Mama, she seemed like a healthy woman, strolling with her family. I rummage through the pockets of the flowered house dress she's wearing. And we're like the last family portrait: Papa with my brother in his arms, and Mama holding my hand.

Before the baby is born, her mother cries over anything, and after he dies, she stops crying. And even though Doctor Yarcho said she'd get better, I saw her enter a place where, perhaps, she is no one. She'd rest against the goose down pillows, and barely open her eyes to complain, "Something hurts here."

"Cry," Papa would tell her.

I see two shadows on her bed: one of her head, elongated on the wall by the light of the lamp, and the other, the shadow of her shadow.

And the girl tells herself there is something in those light violet eyes that still search and plead.

One day, taking advantage of the good mood Bobe was in because a farmer had paid everything he owed her, the girl asks what is wrong with her mother. Bobe does not answer, but the girl insists until she finally says, "*Tzures.*"

"What are they?"

"Tzures are tzures," she responded, sadly.

There was something cruel in that word.

The girl sees her mother hanging clothes. And I raise the pole, making the diapers sway in the breeze. It's neither nighttime nor daytime. It's foggy, the mist is gray, and the rain falls endlessly.

Later, after her mother dies, the girl will try to convince herself that her mother is still alive. She walks with empty eyes, like her mother, wandering all through the house in the pale, white light, but it is hard to be so sick, as sick as her mother. She hears her mother talking to the son she no longer has.

She used to walk down the hall, and I'd spy on her while she turned on the lights of the house, looking for my brother, and Bobc, following discreetly, two steps behind Mama, would turn them off.

The light in the room is dim, and from where she watches, everything has another thickness, another texture. She spies on the girl, she spies on her mother, and recognizes both of them.

The girl peers at the sky through the window: there is a lunar eclipse. She pretends it was she, and not her brother, who died. She stretches out on the cold tiles, with her eyes closed, motionless, evoking death and thinking about her own death, and the girl is her mother, and says, "Oh, look how pale my little girl is, and how she sleeps!" And she can see her mother leaning over her, sad. The girl believes the dead go out into the darkness, when no one sees them, and they look into the eyes of the living with a secret longing. And when fear seeps into her bones, the light seems to fade, and she sees something no one sees: her own memory.

JOURNAL 3

She says she will not end up buried in this town, and asks her daughter to close the shutters so that she may see in the darkness what the light keeps her from seeing.

The sky is stormy, and Papa's at his desk in the living room, sitting in his swivel chair. He's working on something with his glasses on. The clock on the wall strikes eleven.

It is nighttime, and the girl's shadow is outlined by the glow of the lamp. Her mother sees rats, and the girl assures her that she has smashed them with the broom. Her father gives her mother a pill that takes away her pain.

My shadow is the one who makes me say that I found Mama at dawn, naked in the hall, with her hair all messed up. But I remember it was later that morning when I put a nightgown on her and she murmured that a snake had latched onto her nipple while she was sleeping.

No one in the house explains to the girl what is wrong with her mother, but she need only look at her to figure it out.

I told Bobe that Mama was like that because my brother had died. She raised her hands to her head, cried out to God, and made me promise to never say that again.

The girl is in her room, looking out the window toward the Brener house. There is barely a breeze. She thinks her friend Sofía must be asleep. A passenger train goes rushing by, and she hears Bobe shout, and her father scream, "Lete got out!"

Papa runs in the night, and catches up with Mama not too far from the house, on the bank by the railroad tracks. Mama returns in Papa's arms, and looks at me in a strange way. There's something about her that isn't quite right. . . .

As Bobe raises the blinds in the shop, the girl calls her and says her mother has fainted by the front door, and her grandmother shouts, "Lete, Lete!"

I go get water, and from the kitchen I hear Bobe say, "Oh my God, child, you're pregnant again."

And when I return, I ask Bobe if it's true Mama's going to have a baby, and she asks me where I got that idea. Bobe tells me about the time when she was my age, and lived in Odessa, and describes a tree called *pes*. I listen to her, even though I'm sleepy, and when she asks me if I'm paying attention, I tell her yes. Then Bobe tells me that when she escaped the pogrom, she carried the seeds of that tree to Lyon, and then brought them on the boat to plant here, but her brother threw them into the sea.

That night the girl dreams that a man walks into her room wearing a raincoat with the collar turned up, and tells her, with a cigarette in his mouth, to come with him. She follows him down a long hall to a dark, silent room at the other end. Her father is there, and when he sees her, he says, "Baby, horses can do whatever they want, but not little girls."

I opened my eyes. I thought about the man in the dream, and I don't know why I saw Bobe cutting calla lilies by the spigot, and the soapy water running down the trench, carrying a peacock feather away.

Even today I see that scene, and Bobe remains in that spot, cutting lilies next to the dripping spigot, and the water carries away a peacock feather.

Doctor Yarcho's with Mama, and Papa asks me to go with him to buy cigarettes. I tell him I know Mama's going to have another baby, and he says not anymore.

Papa buys me a chocolate bar, and we go home.

One afternoon when the girl is walking home with León, she sees her father leaving the Dutchman's boarding house with a woman who has curly hair, like her mother.

"That's your father," León says.

"No, that's not him," the girl replies.

That night, after dinner, her father asks her to make him a cup of tea.

"How much sugar?"

"Two lumps."

He looks at her with tired eyes and says, "Is something wrong, Déborah?"

The girl looks at him, but does not ask him anything, not a thing. She only says, "Your cigarette went out."

Her father no longer has the same voice, and she no longer has the voice of the child she once was.

One afternoon I ran into Papa with that woman.

"Déborah, I'd like you to meet . . . " Papa said.

I looked at that woman, then turned and ran away.

Every time I think about that other woman, I'm afraid I'll meet her again. My eyes didn't want to see her, and I asked Aunt Berta who that woman was standing behind me, and Aunt Berta gave me a strange look.

The fog is thick. The girl crosses the square with her father, and glances at him every now and then, and sees that his eyes are bloodshot. She asks him where they are going, and holds onto his arm as the two of them walk in silence. They take a shortcut down a path, and when they get to the sidewalk, she sees old Mr. Slavin, engrossed in the newspaper he is reading under an awning. The streets are nearly deserted, and the air is damp and cold. They walk through the market, which smells of herring. Then they come to the railroad tracks, and a train passes by, with a man hanging from the steps of the caboose. The noise of the engine drowns out her father's words. "I'm leaving tomorrow."

Her father speaks of someone, of something, "I used to be different before . . ."

He chokes and cannot stop coughing. When the coughing spell passes, the girl tells him not to talk anymore.

"It's going to start pouring down rain," he says. And we run home.

Papa's packing his suitcase. He keeps looking at his watch, and I go over to him and plead, "Papa, don't leave," but he says nothing, and then I know he's going away.

Her father closes the suitcase, and when the girl hears the horn of the taxi that is waiting for him, she begs him again to stay, and he hugs her. He leaves, and everything is a long silence.

The girl goes to her room and writes in a journal. She writes a story that never ends. Then she hides the journal behind a drawer of the armoire. She hides it from herself.

Many years will pass before she can remember that moment she thought was forgotten.

It's raining all over Entre Ríos. The taxi driver, who's taking me to the cemetery, says we'll get there in an hour. I ask him if we might get stuck in the mud, with all the rain, and he tells me not to worry.

Anything can happen, and silently I tell myself that I once knew all that's coming back to me now. I recognize the thicket along the roadside, the bridge over Malo Creek, the cows grazing in everlasting boredom, the horse-drawn cart that comes to a halt now, the smell of rotting flesh, and the fog.

I thought Papa wasn't going to return, but he did. He asks me where Bobe is, and when I tell him she's not here, he says, "Leave me alone with Mama."

I saw Papa leave Mama's room. The ring of keys jingled in his hand. Mama hadn't forgiven him.

"Stop seeing her, Papa."

"I already have."

Nearly forty years have passed, and the more the image of those I loved fades away, the less I'm able to rebuild the space where I was born, and yet, the desire to reconstruct every moment lived in my house persists, like the echo those memories left in me.

They're still there in the family portrait that was never taken: Papa, with my brother in his arms, and Mama, holding my hand. I can hear Papa's shallow breath. And I strain to hear the rumble of what once was, and I catch fleeting glimpses, like remains on a battlefield.

Papa and Mama are still *there*, although *there* no longer exists anywhere. They're dead, but their voices reverberate, unexpectedly. I close my eyes and I see them: Papa, deep in thought, and Mama, floating in her bed, as if in an ark, and although Bobe's in her shop, she'll soon come into Mama's room to put ice on her head.

Mama tells Papa, "Straighten your shawl, or the people going with us to the cemetery will say you're a *shleper*."

Mama asks them to help her. The pain in her head is unbearable. She says, "Morphine," and then says she doesn't want to live, that she only wants to sleep. And Papa holds her and gives her a pill. When Mama falls asleep, Papa leaves the room and screams, his voice hoarse and his lungs destroyed by tobacco, "God damn it!"

Papa grimaces, and then mutters, "At least I can curse God for this."

Bobe hears him, and shouts that all Communists are from hell, and that God will punish them. And Papa yells at her, "God doesn't exist! If he did, you wouldn't be here. Do you even know who I am? You don't know, old woman. You're afraid, and you don't even know what you're afraid of. . . . Just shut up, old woman!"

It is the first time the girl has seen her father so angry. She worries that when her mother wakes up, she will be hungry, so she tells Bobe not to forget to make her something to eat. Before the girl goes into the kitchen, she scoops rainwater into a bucket.

The girl dips her head into the basin, and her hair floats on the water, straight and shiny.

It is nighttime again, and once more her mother's shouts can be heard. The girl does not want to hear her. All that screaming wears her out, and she cannot stand it. She cannot bear the night. She wraps her hair in a towel, and then combs it out as the moon rises over the eucalyptus trees.

I tremble, watching through the window as the full moon rises. I tremble when I hear Mama say my brother didn't die, repeating it until she loses her voice. I tremble when I look at the bed where she lay submerged. Suddenly, she shouts that we're sick, "Very sick."

At night, her mother searches for her son all through the house, in the rooms and down the hallway. She writes on her bedroom wall with lipstick, "Bring him back to me."

That night the girl dreams that the man in the raincoat is taking her away to a foreign country. He pierces her with angry looks, and tells her that he is going to abandon her there, far away. The girl knows that the man knows that she pretends not to see him, but at that moment she wakes up.

The girl sees her father in a train car. She wants to go with him, but a woman is in the compartment tending to his suitcase, and the girl is frightened and stands still, looking at them. The woman drops her head on her father's chest, and closes her eyes.

"Leave, Déborah," I tell myself, but I can't leave, because Papa's stroking that woman's neck, and I see his hand moving down. I want to board, but you're not allowed to get on or off the train while it's moving, so I run along the platform, and the train pulls away. And the girl I once was sits down on a bench in the waiting room and doesn't cry.

The girl returns home, walking down an alley, and when she comes through the doorway, Bobe tells her that she has mud on her shoes, but she does not listen. She is traveling with the man who is riding on the train.

She goes out to the patio in her bare feet. The air is laden with the scent of fennel and the chirping of locusts. The girl walks over to the well and sees a melancholy face that grows longer and longer in the water.

Mama called for me to come fluff up her pillow so that she could complain about the pain tormenting her. She said the pain in her head was piercing her brain.

I need to return to her grave and tell her, as if I were a girl, what I didn't tell her back then, that even though I wasn't her only child, I was her only daughter, and I knew that my brother wasn't the only one whose death had destroyed her. But I also knew the memory of my brother's death was what led her to swallow the pills that day.

I see lightning behind the chinaberry trees, and I hear Bobe tell me to bundle up so I don't catch a cold. She says the new year's coming, and she's going to make potato *kigl* with goose fat. I tell her that she's making my mouth water, and I laugh and think about saving a piece for León, and I remember the lemon drop passing from his mouth to mine. Once again, I hear wailing, and I'm not sure if Mama's moaning out of pleasure or pain.

The mist envelops the house, and it is as if the house never existed. The wind begins to blow fiercely, carrying the mist away, and suddenly the house appears in the open. The wind crashes against the old walls, penetrating them and whistling.

One morning the girl helps her mother out of bed, and watches her as she stares at her face in the mirror. She asks the girl if things are going well in the shop, and she mentions the money they owe the Lucienville Co-Op.

"What did she say?" Bobe asks me.

I tell her Mama wants stewed apples. Her mother twists her mouth, trying to smile.

Bobe tells Mama that she has to bathe her. Mama's pale, with circles under her eyes, and you can see her ribs. Bobe lathers her armpits, back, and breasts, and murmurs, "I'm getting too old for this." She says her back hurts, and as she reaches for her daughter's pubis, she pauses when she sees the girl and tells her that she should leave.

The steam covering the purple tiles doesn't evaporate. I open the shutters and tell myself it's the first time the sun's been out in a long time, and once again I'm on the patio of my house. I go into the kitchen and see Bobe sprinkling flour on the table, with her back to me. Then she flattens the dough with a rolling pin and kneads it, telling me it's going to rain again. I'm the one who goes out to the patio and takes down the sheets. I say that they're dry now, and as I lay them over my shoulder, a bolt of lightning pierces the sky, and I hear Bobe singing:

> *Au clair de la lune,*
> *Mon ami Pierrot!*
> *Prête-moi ta plume*
> *pour écrire un mot.*
> *Ma chandelle est morte,*
> *Je n'ai plus de feu . . .*

The girl stares at herself in the mirror, naked. She is slender, with budding breasts, and her pubis is covered in soft hair. She has bled for the first time. Her mother tells her she will bleed every month, and that she is a woman now.

Sofía's my best friend, and I tell her about Mama's problems, but when she asks me what's wrong with her, I don't know what to tell her, so I say she's still in mourning.

Déborah plays cards with Sofía. Every so often, the shadow of her sick mother passes before her eyes, and she thinks, "My

brother's death seems to be the only thing that matters to her."
When was the last time the girl rested her head on her mother's
chest, and her mother caressed her?

I place the seven of hearts on the table, and then put down my
hand of cards and tell Sofía I have to leave, and I go home.

The girl walks into her house and hears a moan, and then a
longer one, coming from her parents' room. She stands still until
she hears nothing more. Then she calls her mother. Her father
cracks open the door and tells her not to bother them, that they
are sleeping. She gets a glimpse of her mother naked, pulling up
the sheet to cover herself. She knows what they are doing from
Sofía, who learned about it from Angélica, who works as a servant
in her house. Sofía says it hurts the first time, and you bleed like
you do with your period. Angélica says that afterward, you feel like
doing it again.

The girl knows why there was something dark in her father's
eyes when he said, "We're sleeping," and she also knows that her
brother did not arrive in the long beak of any white bird.

She returns to her friend's house and tells her what she saw.
She stretches out on the bed and, with her eyes closed, says that
one day she will do it too.

"When you get married," Sofía says.

That afternoon Déborah says she does not want to end up a
spinster, like Aunt Berta. She says it in a fit of passion she cannot
repress, and the two girls laugh.

The scene with Sofía plays over and over. I walk into the
house, and Bobe asks me where I've been. And there's the smell
that reminds me of my grandmother: borscht soup.

Bobe tells me, "Eat, dear." Before I finish the last spoonful, she
puts more beet soup in my bowl.

The red broth is steaming now, as it steamed before, amid
the bellowing cries of the Cossacks and the clash of their sabers,
when the girl who was my bobe hid outside her house. She asks
her grandmother to teach her how to make borscht, and Bobe, her

eyes dancing with joy, tells her how to prepare it so the borscht turns out delicious.

Bobe teaches me to make borscht soup. The broth steams in the pot, and the aroma of the snowy steppe rises in that big silver ladle. Bobe says you can eat it cold with cream, but I like it to reach my belly hot, and while I savor it, I ask her if it's true that there's life after death. My question irritates and exasperates her. It makes her suffer, as if I'd betrayed her, and she swears on our only God that there's no resurrection for those who have already died.

I gaze at the field of flax through the taxi window, and tell myself it seems like the sea when it's blue, and I look again at the photograph I'm holding, where Mama looks young and beautiful, still a little girl, with the same light violet eyes, in the sailor suit Bobe made especially for that portrait, and I tell myself this is the last image of Mama I still have. Perhaps I can go back to when she was a young girl and hear, as if I were there, the rumors of her engagement, and also Bobe forbidding Mama to see her fiancé, and perhaps I can see her obeying her mother, with the meekness and passivity that will lead to her ruin.

JOURNAL 4

"**B**obe, the electricity went out," the girl says. Her grandmother calls the electric company, but no one answers. In the shadowy darkness, she removes the globe from the gas lantern, lights the wick, and pumps until the flame rises.

Bobe gets the sewing basket and tells the girl that she wants to shorten the hem of her dress. She tries to thread the needle in the dim light, but cannot do it, and grumbles, "I won't allow my granddaughter to run around like some black farm girl."

The girl is about to respond, but when she sees her grandmother's cold glare, she stops and kicks the chair, making it fall over with a loud crash.

While Bobe waters the blooming jonquils and larkspur, the girl walks behind her. When her grandmother notices her, she puts down the watering can and says, "Not in your bare feet, my dear."

"It's hot, Bobe. . . ."

"That doesn't matter."

There is not much light in the kitchen. Bobe looks at the girl endearingly and runs her fingers through her bangs. The girl rests her elbows on the table and her head in her hands, and says that she is tired. Bobe sees how much she has grown, and says in a hushed voice, "You'll always be *mein kind* to me."

Then Bobe asks me if I like a certain boy. When I say yes, she asks, "Is it León?"

It does not matter if they are open or closed: she does not see anything, she cannot see a thing, not up close, nor far away. She waits.

Her father develops photographs in the late afternoon. The girl knows that when he leaves the station wagon parked on the street and closes the garage, sealing it with black paper, the developing ceremony is about to begin.

Papa would place the negative in the enlarger, project the light over the glossy paper, and submerge it into each of the trays that contained the developing solutions. As the faces and bodies of his fellow Party members began to emerge, he'd put down his cigarette and say to me, "There are details, Déborah, that get lost," and to my amazement, he'd tear up the photo and develop it again. I liked to keep him company under the light of the red bulb, secluded there, far away from the world.

One afternoon the girl finds a photograph of a woman, which still smells of acetic acid. The woman has large breasts, and is the same one who got on the train with her father, the same one who came out of the Dutchman's boarding house with him. The girl tries to remember at what moment her father screamed at her, "Déborah, what are you doing?" but she only recalls the torn photograph of the woman in her hands, and her father's eyes staring at her, waiting for her to speak. She looked down, and her father told her to leave.

The girl goes into the shop, and Bobe tells her that only a man like her father could waste time in that darkroom with those sickening smells. She hears her grandmother say she is not going to let that *muzhik* stink up her house anymore, but the girl knows her grandfather used to develop photographs too. Bobe says, "Puttering around in that dingy room is the only thing your father knows how to do."

She says Communists like being in the dark, without realizing that the girl's father is listening to her. Then Bobe notices him, and looks at him, unperturbed. Suddenly, he grabs her arm and twists it until she cries out, and he screams at her, "Keep your mouth shut, damn it!"

Bobe swears at him, and he lets go of her, and at that moment, the girl hears her mother shout, "Just let me die!" and she runs to her side. Mama tells me that ever since we snatched my brother away from her, she can't feel her feet. I see her face bathed in a strange light as she searches for him. She touches her thighs, and her bare legs, then puts her hands between them and rubs there.

Bobe shakes the girl and screams that she is upsetting her mother. The girl complains that no one talks to her about her mother's illness. Her father collapses into the living room armchair, resting his head in his hands. Something inside him erupts, brutally, and he blurts out what is wrong with her mother, and she shrinks away, frightened, not wanting to understand.

The girl goes out to the garden and vomits over the calla lilies, next to the dripping spigot.

Her father walks on the patio, calmly, and tells the girl that her mother was the most beautiful woman from her village.

Mama inherited a defect that's deep inside my body now. . . . I'm not going to have children. . . .

Everything becomes blurred next to the lilies, and a confusing, wild clamor keeps ringing inside her, pounding her.

The girl has seen her father with that other woman, laughing at everything and nothing.

Her father asks, "Déborah, what's wrong with you?"

She goes over to the window. How can her father caress that woman's hair, and her large breasts, breasts like her mother's?

To her father, she is still a little girl, and even though she menstruates, he does not want to know about it, and if perhaps he does know, he prefers to think he does not. He asks her again what is wrong, and she tells him not to ask her because it embarrasses her. Her father says nothing; he barely speaks anymore, as if he were hiding something, or himself, as if he were vanishing along with the cigarette that smolders in his mouth. Later, the girl goes outside to the deserted street. It is not dark yet.

We eat dinner, then I serve tea. Bobe tells me to change my blouse, that she can see right through it, and with that blouse on, I look like a whore.

Bobe sits in the wicker chair and hears on the radio that the railroad strike is going to continue, and that there are infiltrators in the strike.

"They'll kill each and every one of them," she says.

Papa pretends not to hear her. I shudder, and tell him there are no "infiltrators" in town, as Bobe calls the striking railroad workers.

Off in the distance someone sings:

> *See saw, see saw*
> *the carpenters of San Juan,*
> *ask for bread, are given none,*
> *ask for cheese, are given bones,*
> *and their necks get cut or wrung . . .*

The light dwindles. The girl looks at her father, who seems sad, and she holds his hand and says, "When I was little, I used to be afraid, and would close my eyes to hide."

"What were you afraid of?"

"Afraid that . . . Mama's afraid that the police will take you away, and I . . ."

I don't think Papa's seeing that woman anymore. He spends more time at home, when he's not working or going to Party meetings. I think Bobe knows Papa was running around with that woman, but I never heard her talk about it.

Outside the air is scorching, but not inside the house, with its tall ceilings and thick walls. The girl peeks through the blinds and sees a young woman dressed in a tight skirt and white shoes. The girl figures she must be waiting for her grandmother to open the shop. Bobe tells her that girl is a whore, and that she refuses to give her even one more yard of fabric on credit. She opens the door and shouts, "You either pay me, or I'll turn you in, Rosa."

"I'll pay you back when the mill workers get paid at the end of the month, Bobe Enya."

"If your mother could see you, may she rest in peace. Just look at yourself—you're not even thirty yet, and you've already lost your teeth."

The girl listens and sees that Rosa lowers her head and says nothing, while Bobe chastises her, "When your mama used to come here to do the laundry, she'd bring you along, and I remember you were an obedient and respectful little girl. But my how you've changed, Rosa. You can't fool me. Your little ones must be starving, and there you go getting yourself pregnant like a rabbit."

Bobe shuts the door in her face, and I hear Rosa scream at her, "Fucking Jew!"

The heat is suffocating, so Bobe opens her shop later than usual. The girl feels sad, sitting on the front steps of the house. She has not spoken to León for days.

"Come now, it's not so bad, *mein kind*," her grandmother says to her.

The girl thinks about León, that he is not going to call her. Suddenly, Bobe says, "Look who's here." And when she looks up, she sees León next to her.

"I want to show you the camera they gave me," León tells her.

At that moment, the girl sees a policeman entering the shop, and hears him say to her grandmother that he did not see her at Sheine Malke's funeral. Then he asks, "Have you heard anything about the strike?"

"I'm not interested in politics."

"But your son-in-law is very well informed, my dear lady. . . ."

I see Bobe's hands trembling, and the policeman leaves, and I look at her, frightened, and she says it's not worth it to be afraid, and tells me León's waiting for me.

I don't know if what I saw then is what I see now. It's as if the past had reopened a wound. I still have the scar. It's a cold, white line that runs crosswise along the palm of my hand, and when I look at it, I see Papa again, sitting in the shade of the grape arbor. The erysipelas left scars on his face and lesions on his neck and nose. And the memory of Papa speeds past my eyes like a gust of wind, banging the shutters, and there I am, sitting on an apple crate, listening to him tell me the story of a white whale. Papa has his raincoat on, with the collar turned up, and a cigarette in his mouth.

Papa's Tony Reseck in *I'll Be Waiting*.

The girl cannot wait to see her father, and when he comes in, she will run to his arms and wrap her thin frame, little arms, and short legs around his tall body. Her father says, "My girl," and she knows that she would lose her mind without him.

Her father's voice is calm. He seems to know what is happening to his daughter.

"My love," he says to her. And for a moment she forgets everything. He takes a fountain pen from his shirt pocket and gives it to her.

I write in my diary with the fountain pen Papa gave me, "I don't think Papa's left that woman, even though he says he has."

Papa put his hand on my forehead and said, "You're burning up with fever."

And he called Doctor Yarcho. The doctor saw spots of pus on my throat, and said I had diphtheria. And when he said "diphtheria," I realized what I had was very serious.

Bobe took care of me as only she knew how, and Papa brought me books.

I couldn't swallow, and Doctor Yarcho asked me how old I was, and I said twelve, and he told me to say "aaah," and I answered, "Twe . . . eel . . . ve." My fever broke after a few days, and I was hungrier than I'd ever been before.

Doctor Yarcho asked me if it was true I wanted to be a photographer, and I told him I didn't know.

Everything draws near or fades away, depending on the time of day, and the diffusion of the light.

Mama sleeps nearly all day, and I stay by her side, reading *Alice's Adventures in Wonderland*. The girl will read that book again many times. She knows entire paragraphs by heart:

> "Who are *you*?" said the Caterpillar.
> This was not an encouraging opening for a conversation. Alice replied, rather shyly, "I . . . I hardly know, sir, just at present . . . at least I know who I was when I got up this morning, but I think I must have been changed several times since then. . . ."

The girl sees her mother open her eyes and speak to her father, as if she were his mother, and to Bobe, as if she were her sister, saying, "Tell me what I did to deserve this." Then she screams, "Why do you make me suffer like this?"

When Mama's shouts penetrate the walls of the house and can be heard beyond the train station, I see that Papa doesn't know what to do with himself, and I hear Bobe say, "I can't take it anymore."

The girl is surprised to see that for the first time her father and grandmother agree about something. They say Mama should be hospitalized in Buenos Aires. They say she'll be taken care of there, and I can go see her. They say she'll get better.

The girl opens the book to the page her father had marked:

> She was fast asleep.
>
> Gabriel, leaning on his elbow, looked for a few moments unresentfully on her tangled hair and half-open mouth, listening to her deep-drawn breath. So she had had that romance in her life: a man had died for her sake. . . . One by one they were all becoming shades. Better pass boldly into that other world, in the full glory of some passion, than fade and wither dismally with age. . . .*

Whenever a train passes, shaking the walls of the house, Bobe locks Mama in her room so that she can't escape. Bobe says Mama's stronger now than before she got sick, and she can't handle her anymore. I spy through the keyhole, and see that Mama's frightened, and when the train goes away, she sings, "*Je le sais, tout casse, Tout lasse et tout passe: Les châteaux, les châsses, Tout ce que l'on brasse, Ou que l'on tasse. . . .*"

The darkness, the fadeout, like a black night, will begin shortly before the girl enters the stage, and will end much later, when the girl is a woman.

Bobe hires a nurse and tells me, "I don't want anyone to know."

"But what if they ask me?"

"No one will ask you anything."

It is always the girl who remains silent, so that no one in town says a word about her mother. "Don't say anything, Déborah."

---

* James Joyce, "The Dead," in *The Dubliners* (1914; repr. New York: Penguin, 1993).

I only tell myself what's happening with Mama. I don't say anything to myself about me, only about Mama. Bobe and Papa impose silence, repeating to me the words they say over and over, "Don't say anything, Déborah."

The May afternoon seems caught between the hazy sun, peeking in and out, and the night that has not yet fallen. The girl hears noises, as if someone were grinding glass, and then she sees the inevitable.

Mama destroyed paintings and photographs, and pushed over the cupboard, with the set of dishes, and the china closet, with Bobe's crystal, and there are pieces of porcelain and glass scattered everywhere. I get the broom and sweep them up.

It was not easy for the nurse and Bobe to get her into bed. Her mother leans over that space next to her bed, as if her son were in his cradle, and calls his name.

The girl thinks about what she cannot understand. Words are not like the dead, who can be covered up with dirt.

The nurse tied Mama to the bed with leather straps and took care of the wounds on her wrists. Then she gave her an injection to put her to sleep.

Papa and Bobe were speaking in Yiddish, in that anxious way they had of talking to each other. In Yiddish they know everything, but in Spanish they say only stupid things.

Papa paces around the room, bows his head and stops, then paces some more. Bobe gets exasperated. "Stay still, will you?"

Papa murmurs something I can't hear, goes to the refrigerator, and eats something, and then puts a toothpick between his teeth, as he usually did, and sinks into the armchair.

Ever since they increased the dosage of morphine, her mother wakes up calmly. Still doped, she smiles and seems to welcome the day, humming, *"Adiós muchachos."* And the girl thinks her mother is dying.

"What are you thinking about, *mein kind*?" Bobe asks me.

"Nothing," I say, even though I was thinking about the people who talked about Mama and Papa, and about me too.

"What can you expect from a girl with a crazy mother and a Commie father?" That's what I heard, the girl with the crazy mother and the Commie father, wherever the Jews and Gentiles got together, those greedy lovers of good business deals and profitable marriages.

León looks at me, and I ask him why he's staring at me, and he says my braids are beautiful. He gives me a letter and tells me to read it when I get home.

The girl wants to conceal in the darkness what she overheard. She turns her back on what people say. She looks out the window and hears the storm, but does not cover her eyes. She waits for it.

The rain falls so hard it floods the house, and all around I see wet walls and the water stain above the baseboards. And I think I hear Bobe saying, "The stork will come through the transom."

And Papa appears in his raincoat, with the collar turned up, and tells me, "You're going to stay with Aunt Berta. We're taking your mother to Buenos Aires."

Bobe says they'll give her a treatment there to help her get better. She tells me she doesn't know how to say in Spanish what they'll do to her.

"Are they going to operate on her head?" the girl asks.

No one dares say yes, no one dares say no. She asks again, "What are they going to do to Mama?"

The space becomes deserted, silent. I hear rapid footsteps, and a door opening and closing again. Papa and Bobe look at each other. The loud footsteps resonate throughout my body, along with Papa's voice, and confused whispers in the darkness.

The girl goes into her mother's room and sees the nurse taking off the restraints. When she sees me, Mama asks me for the bedpan.

The nurse tells her that she can't use the bedpan, that she has to get up to go to the bathroom. Mama says, "I'm not going with the woman in white." The nurse tells her that the girl will go with her.

Mama sits there with her feet dangling over the bed. Her light violet eyes look at me, distantly. I see the fragile strands of her hair and a slenderness that frightens me.

"I feel much better."

For a moment, the girl believes what her mother says; at that moment, she needs to believe. Her mother slips off the bed, looks around, and walks slowly to the bathroom.

The nurse tells her, "Don't close the door, Lete."

Mama sits down on the toilet and smiles at me, runs her hand over her face, and declares, "I like it in here!"

The taxi leaves the gravel road and turns onto a narrow muddy road where the only things in sight are grazing cows. The driver stays in the tracks, and at one point the wheels of the car slide, and he curses the road, and that curse reminds her that she has never left her land. In the murky light, she sees that the road to the cemetery is the same as before, and she tells herself it has not stopped raining since she left.

JOURNAL 6

I found Mama sitting in front of her dressing table mirror, putting on red lipstick. When she noticed me, she asked me to bring her the knitting needles. She said Aunt Berta deserved a better husband than the one she had, and acting as if she were Aunt Berta, she spoke to her husband with harsh words, then looked under the bed and said, "I always worry about what goes on under here."

Then, as if Aunt Berta were with her, she said, "That low-down husband of yours," and mumbled, "*Pas pour moi, je te répète Berta, oh l'amour, tu sais, le corps, l'amour, la mort, ces trois ne font qu'un, n'est-ce pas?*"

Now I see Mama pick up the thermometer from the nightstand and put it in her mouth. The nurse takes it away from her, and Mama spits on her and tries to scratch her. When she manages to hold her down, Mama sticks out her tongue and licks the nurse's face.

"Quick, help me!" the nurse shouts at me.

The girl puts the strap around her mother's legs and fastens it to the bed frame. Her mother screams at them to let her loose. She screams until the morphine puts her to sleep.

I went out to the sidewalk, and the fresh air from the street was a caress I'll never forget. I walked to the square, and everyone looked at me, as if I'd done something I shouldn't have. I crossed the path to the other side of the railroad crossing. The train coming from Asunción went by, and the passengers put their arms out the windows and waved. They were traveling to somewhere I wished I could go.

The nurse took off Mama's straps and before she left she told me, "With the dose of morphine I gave her, she'll sleep quite a while."

Mama slept a long time, then moved her arms and head, opened her eyes, and asked me if I was León's mother. When I said no, she mumbled something I couldn't understand.

The girl goes over to her mother and caresses her forehead, but when she tries to hug her, her mother screams not to touch her, that she hates being touched. She waits for her mother to calm down. She closes her eyes and thinks, "I'd like to go to a place where no one knows me." When she opens her eyes, the girl sees that her mother, who has soiled herself in bed, gets up with her hands covered in shit, grabs the knitting needles, and threatens to stick herself in the eyes.

The nurse manages to strap her down. The girl runs to get Bobe, but her grandmother is busy with a client and says she will talk to her later.

"There's no need to get excited, *mein kind*," Bobe says.

"I'm not a child," says the girl, "not anymore."

"Why don't you go straighten your room."

The girl writes in her journal:

May 21, 1959

It's a gloomy day and Mama's a mess. She crawled on the floor all morning long, and pooped all over herself, and then the nurse had to clean her up and force her back to bed. When the nurse drags her to bed, she looks like a cow being carried off to the butcher.

Papa and Bobe speak to each other in Yiddish all the time. Today I packed my suitcase. . . . I feel like leaving this house forever.

What would I do without you?

Oh, I forgot to tell you, yesterday I found a little gray kitten by the fence, still as could be, and freezing to death. I knew I couldn't keep him, so I took the kitten to León so that he'd take care of him.

The girl closes her journal and hides it behind a drawer so that no one can read it.

She goes back to the shop. With a raspy voice, Bobe orders her to do something, I can't remember what, and the girl screams, "You can't tell me what to do. . . . You're nobody!"

Bobe grabs the girl by the hair and drags her to her room, saying, "How dare you talk back to your grandmother like that! You're going to turn out just like your father. . . . You're going to kill me!"

When he came in, Papa asked Bobe, "Did Lete take her medicine?"

"What Yarcho gave her doesn't calm her down."

The rest of the day Bobe did more than usual. And although she was normally in a bad mood, that day she was particularly unbearable. She got into it with me, and then with Papa, and when she realized that neither of us reacted to her temper tantrums, she went off grumbling, confused.

"How's my girl?" Papa said, with his hands trembling. "My girl's sad, and I want to see her happy."

"Mama's sick."

"Yes, she's sick."

The girl looks at her father, and he strokes her face. She pats her father's head with her delicate hand and says to him, "You're going bald."

They leave the house, and the girl runs ahead and reaches the railroad crossing before him.

I see Papa returning home without the girl, and I tell myself, "He's talking to himself; he's happy. Maybe he could be happy once in a while."

I brush my hair, and call for Bobe to braid it. Aunt Berta says she'll do it, and Bobe lets her fix my hair.

I keep Aunt Berta company while she waits for the train to Nogoyá.

She sees the girl wearing braids, seated next to Aunt Berta, on a bench in the waiting room at the Basavilbaso train station. It is raining.

Bobe didn't allow Mama to marry her boyfriend because he wasn't Jewish. And then we walk along the platform until Aunt Berta boards the train. Standing on the step, she buttons her black wool jacket, covering her large breasts, and tells me as the train pulls out, "After that, your mama became depressed."

The train moves off into the distance.

I shudder when I see the dimly lit lamp, and listen to Mama chew an apple and spit the seeds at my face. I speak to her as you would a child, but she ignores me and asks me to help her find my brother's pacifier. I look for it under the bed, and when I tell her there's nothing there, she screams, "The woman in white, the woman in white hid it from me," until the nurse straps her to the bed frame.

The girl looks at Bobe as she takes her handkerchief from her three-quarter-length sleeve to blow her nose.

At dinnertime, Bobe cries and says she doesn't have the strength to go on. Papa tells her something he never said before: "A woman like you can't give up. . . . Lete needs you, your granddaughter needs you."

And Bobe looks at me with tears in her eyes, and hugs me. Then she looks at Papa, but she can't speak. Papa says in a low voice, "You're strong," and when Bobe calms down, they talk as if they'd always gotten along.

Early that morning, Mama swallowed a bottle of barbiturates, but no one could explain exactly when she took them. Bobe said the nurse wasn't watching her, and she pounded her chest, saying, "How could I have trusted that *shvarze*?"

"Be quiet, the nurse will hear you," Papa said.

"I'm not going to be quiet," Bobe answered.

Just then, the nurse came out and said they were going to pump Mama's stomach, and when she opened the door to go back into the room, I caught a glimpse of Mama with a tube up her nose.

Doctor Yarcho said he'd pumped her stomach, and we just had to wait and see.

After a while, the girl goes into the room and hears her mother snoring under the oxygen tent. She seems thin, but she is still her mother.

A rancid smell filled the room, and in the midst of that stupor, Mama was snoring. I looked at her dresses, hanging in the armoire, the pads for her period, and a few objects: a powder box, a powder puff, a hairbrush, and a bottle of brilliantine, and I thought all those things were horrible.

Doctor Yarcho said there was nothing more he could do. Papa told me I should leave.

I saw the leaves from the oak tree that's in front of my house. They were brown, and some were on the ground. I picked up a leaf and pasted it in my journal.

The girl remembers the hateful look on her mother's face when she came into the room with the oak leaves she had gathered for her.

The girl records in her journal:

Her body stiffened, and Mama resisted when Bobe tried to put the pill between her teeth, but she made her swallow it. I watched as Bobe stuck the needle right through her underwear, without a warning, and Mama scratched her, and me too, and I did whatever she wanted me to do, so long as I didn't have to look at those eyes of hers, like a cow in agony.

I didn't say anything when she hit me, I just listened to her laughing. It wasn't just my brother's death that made her like this. No. I asked Aunt Berta why Mama was this way, but she didn't answer.

Bobe cried and kept asking, "Why, *mein kind*?" and I didn't know what to say.

The nurse comes into the room with a towel and closes the door. Bobe and Papa follow her. The girl hears footsteps coming and going. Bobe shouts, "No!" and she's afraid of that scream, and Papa comes out of Mama's room and embraces the girl without saying a word to her.

The girl gets out of bed and goes to the kitchen, where she hears Bobe say they are going to give the corpse the ritual bath. When she hears the word "corpse," she feels the world disappearing for her.

At home, they didn't want to say Mama had killed herself. They wanted to say she died of a heart attack, but they couldn't. They buried her away from the others, with the suicides.

There are a lot of people at Mama's wake. Aunt Berta serves coffee. No one talks about Mama to me. They say I'm very pretty, and ask me how I'm doing in school, but they don't mention Mama.

The girl notices that Aunt Berta is talking to a woman whose back is toward her. She tells herself, "She's the same one who came out of the Dutchman's hotel with Papa, the same one who got on the train with him." She asks her aunt who that woman is. Aunt Berta gives her a strange look, and when the woman turns around, the girl sees she is the nurse who took care of her mother.

The procession moved forward over thick mud, and I heard the clatter of the horses' heavy shoes. Low, gray clouds veiled the sky. I saw people spying through their windows. I heard laughter, and looked down, until I felt Aunt Berta's hand on mine.

The girl walks along with her father on one side and Bobe on the other, and her mother goes in front of them, in that wooden coffin.

When she gets home, the girl looks at her mother's empty bed. No traces, no remains. Nothing more than a vast, somber lethargy.

She remembers the photo of the maternal grandfather she never knew, who rests in her memory in the same place he occupied in the house, on the dining room wall. Whenever she looked at the photo of her dead grandfather, she felt both fear and admiration. With his protruding chin, wrinkled forehead, and intense eyes, her grandfather's photo played the role of ogre and wolf in her childhood fantasies.

I turned thirteen a month after Mama died. And that day, I got a shovel and buried the oak leaves that were on the ground, and I said to myself, "No one in the house wished me a happy birthday." I took out my savings and decided to buy myself a little mirror. It was a silly thing that made me happy. But when I gazed at myself, I looked dreadful, and I cried. I'd bought a little mirror for nothing, and felt happy for nothing.

I couldn't stop laughing, just thinking about buying that mirror. It felt good to laugh on my birthday.

JOURNAL 7

I dream that I'm standing in the doorway of my house, and I hear shouts, but I don't want to go in. I'm eleven years old, and my hair is braided down my back.

A man asks me in the language of my grandparents, "Do you know why you're here?" And when I tell him I don't know, the man says I'm there because I killed my brother.

I blink, and then I see a light filtering through a cloud, until the light disappears. I convince myself that I can't see because of exhaustion, and I wait, but it only takes a few minutes to realize that I'm blind.

I grope my way to the window, and when I open it, a gust of wind hits me in the face, and I hear pounding, and think, "Perhaps my nerves are keeping me from seeing. I'm going to lie down until this veil lifts from my eyes. . . ."

I feel like screaming, "Why me?" but I stay still and don't shout. I'm not in pain, I'm not dying, and León loves me.

The whistles of a train. . . . It seems as if I've been blind for an eternity.

I hear the front door, and then León's footsteps as he enters the room and asks me, "D., what are you doing in bed so early?"

I tell him, sobbing, that I can't see a thing, "as if someone had gouged my eyes out, León."

There's a clinic not far from the house, and we go there.

"Let's see, ma'am, tell me what happened."

"All of a sudden, I couldn't see a thing. I thought I couldn't see because I was so exhausted. I saw shapes passing before my eyes, and spots, as if I had a sun inside me, forcing me to stare at it."

"Are you diabetic?"

"No."

"Does anyone in your family have diabetes, any congenital eye malformations, detached retina, keratoconus?"

"No."

"Place your chin here, and don't move or breathe until I tell you."

"All right now, don't blink, and open your eyes wide. Tell me, what do you see?"

"Black."

"Does it hurt?"

"Not now."

"When did it hurt?"

"Before, it was intense."

"Did you hear some bad news?"

"No."

"Do you suffer from hypertension?"

"No."

"This examination doesn't indicate anything, ma'am. Let's do some more tests, and you can come back when the results are in."

León makes me eat. I'm nervous and get upset over the least thing. He tells me to be patient, that the blindness will pass.

How long will I be shut in, closed up in this room, lying in bed like my mother? And what if the blindness doesn't pass?

I get nightmares more and more frequently. A commanding voice asks, "Ladies and gentlemen of the jury, have you reached your verdict?"

"Yes, Your Honor. We declare the defendant guilty in the first degree, and condemn her to death."

"No, I didn't kill him!"

"There's no hope for you," said a dry, strident voice.

I woke up drenched in sweat.

I put two drops of collyrium in each eye, and the cold liquid stings, but I endure it until the burning passes. The time it takes me to get dressed, the time it takes me to find what I'm looking for, is time I don't have.

I try to see that girl who still slips in and out of my memory, in and out, the way I used to glide along the fields of flax, with the wind lifting my skirt, as I watched the sun set. And I tell myself that it's time for the old girl to learn to live with what she has left.

"I have to get back to work."

León helps me organize the photos I took before whatever it is I have happened to me, and I arrange the photos of the voyeurs on cardboard. I run my fingers over the edge of each one, and can recognize what's in each of them by touch.

I have trouble getting around on the streets. León doesn't leave me alone. We go into a bar. There's a pianist there imitating Nat King Cole.

"What would you like to drink, ma'am?" a man asks.

"What do you have . . . ?"

"Joly, bring the lady a glass of *Lucera*."

"*Lucera*," I whisper, and drink it all at once.

I listen to the pianist play *"Manhã de carnaval,"* and for the first time in weeks, I close my eyes, and forget I can't see.

My hand touches León's body between the sheets. He rolls over and tells me to go to sleep.

"I remember when I was on the sidewalk, in front of your house, spinning the hula hoop on my hips, and you couldn't take your eyes off me. Your ears were blood red, and I liked that look on your face. I remember you said our love would last as long as we lived."

"Hold me."

I hold León, and feel something awaken in me at the touch of his skin. He caresses my hips, my breasts. I tell him I want to imagine his eyes. I tell him I don't want the pleasure to ever end, and that I'd like to disappear, naked, embracing him.

I fall asleep.

"Look at them. . . . They're your parents, Déborah."

"Do I see them? No. Not now, León. . . ."

I'm a darkroom behind a camera, trying to capture in the darkness what is inaccessible to my eyes.

Why do I keep imagining a train disappearing in the fog?

I had taken hundreds of photos: of the blind surrounded by the light of day, of the sighted submerged in dirty, gloomy places. I searched their faces for a sign that would make whoever looked at them reflect. Now, I'm the one who's blind.

León buys a bulldog to be my guide. I call him Ulysses. He barks like crazy when I shoot the camera. León says he barks when the flash goes off over his head.

I hear someone speaking Yiddish, and I stop. I ask León to describe that man who's speaking in the language of my grandparents. And he tells me the man is tall, with a beard and sideburns, and that he's wearing thick glasses, a rabbi's hat, and an astrakhan overcoat.

While León describes the man, my eyes remember what they saw, and I think I haven't heard the word "astrakhan" in thirty years. I get the camera ready, setting by touch the depth of field and light, and after calculating the distance that separates me from the rabbi, I shoot.

León tells me the photos of the rabbi turned out well, but my execution is a far cry from what it used to be.

We were eating dinner, and I asked León to pass me the salt. Suddenly, something like a shot went off in my head, and a deluge of memories passed before my eyes: I heard footsteps coming and going, and once again that noise of grinding glass, which made me clench my teeth, and I was frightened. I heard the signalman's bell, and the wind threatening to blow off the metal roof over the patio of my house, and I saw Mama, Papa, and Bobe, standing still, like in a black-and-white photograph. Something gentle, like a forgotten pleasure, came over me, and I felt that fear that takes hold of you in the dark.

Tears burned my eyes, but I wasn't dreaming. There was a flash of light, and I saw León before me.

"Sudden blindness," that's what they said I had.

Now that my eyes can see, I'm going to finish mounting the exhibit of photos revealing that dissatisfied and anxious look of those who seek but do not find what they want to see.

I work day and night organizing the exhibit.

It's been more than three years since I began searching for gazes with the camera. It wasn't easy to find them. There are people who focus on things others don't even notice. Someone who stares like that isn't necessarily a voyeur; they don't always spy on an erotic scene, although they always seem blinded by something they covet. I frame them, and as soon as I have them in my sights, I seize that lascivious gesture that, most of the time, emerges around the mouth, and anticipates that exact gaze I seek. Sometimes, but only once in a while, I manage to capture it.

Undaunted, I shoot them at the most intimate moment of their desire, when their eyes take on a devastating intensity and become one single eye.

I find a boy who cleans a gymnasium where women go to exercise. He has an innocent face, and spends his time on a painter's ladder, cleaning with delight the glass of a skylight that looks down on the locker room. I go there just to photograph him. His eyes peer through the skylight: he doesn't look, he penetrates what he sees.

I've found another: a man in his sixties, who always goes to the same bar around ten in the morning. He drinks coffee, and his eyes peer out over the edge of his cup. I shoot when he takes pleasure in capturing with his gaze a young, blond boy who frequents the bar. His are the most feverish eyes I've ever seen—like something out of *Death in Venice*.

I surprise a woman in the act of seducing a boy. That woman's eyes are those of a dreamer. Later, in a municipal office, I happen to recognize the cashier as the flirt from the bar, but this time she's behind the teller window, and doesn't seduce anyone with her eyes.

I carry her with me in my Pentax.

I get on a bus. There's a girl wearing a miniskirt standing at the far end of the aisle, and there's an old man watching her, voraciously.

The old guy has managed to place a bag at the girl's feet. I move closer, and see that inside the bag there's a camera set to shoot, aiming up her skirt.

I take a picture of a girl who works in a pharmacy on Nueve de Julio Street. Her skin is white, like her hair. When she glances up, I can see her unfathomable eyes and her whiteness. She looks like she could vanish at any moment, but whenever she speaks to a customer, she materializes again. She's not an albino, as one might think. I don't know how many times I shoot her.

Those who have seen the photos of that girl say they can't stop staring at her, and some doubt the girl was ever there, on paper.

On the way to the cemetery, I lose myself again in that passage I read so eagerly as a child:

She was fast asleep.

Gabriel, leaning on his elbow, looked for a few moments unresentfully on her tangled hair and half-open mouth, listening to her deep-drawn breath. So she had had that romance in her life: a man had died for her sake. . . .

I ask the taxi driver for a cigarette. I look at the water and the cattails in the marshes, and I think it's the same water and the same cattails my loved ones saw when they were alive and traveled down this road.

There's a man on the roadside. He has the collar of his raincoat turned up. It's Papa, who passes once more before my eyes, through my memory.

Bobe isn't here, and I start doing my homework and hear a train passing by and Papa yelling to me from the living room, "Make sure your mother doesn't get out!" but it's too late. The door to her room is open, and my heart pounds and my legs tremble. I hear the train whistle and worry, "What if Mama threw herself onto the tracks?" I run through the fog, looking for her, and find her on the embankment lying next to the tracks, eating dirt. When I get closer, Mama looks up at me like a frightened child. With barely a whimper, she lets me take her home.

I put her to bed and all is quiet until I hear Papa's footsteps, and him telling me, "Go on, sweetheart, I'll take care of Mama now."

Now I need to see the images in motion.

I cry for everything I didn't cry for then.

I keep searching for Mama in the fog. Night hasn't fallen completely.

I can't find the words for what I recall. There's something in my memory that comes like a flash of light, something I don't know, and I don't say. And the more I remember, the farther away I seem to be from my childhood, and yet, never before have I felt so close.

I'm not that girl, but I am the girl, all grown up now, who tries to remember. Those hundreds of days, so long ago, have crept back, like shadows extending deep inside me, between sounds and voices that come and go, endlessly.

The taxi driver asks me where I'm from, and I ask him how much farther it is to La Capilla.

"It's called Ingeniero Sajaroff now, ma'am."

I tell him that I know. I know that.

The driver asks me, "Who do you have buried there?"

I tell him to close his window because I'm getting wet. I smell like wet dirt.

The driver tells me that the phosphorescence rising from the ground, way off on the horizon, is a ghostly light.

As the morning passes, I hear confusing noises and see three fleeting figures burst in the air and then vanish.

I know there are just a few more miles to the cemetery. I look out the window and the trees seem to move. They're the only thing that remained, and they're all there, the eucalyptus trees. When I get to the cemetery, I'm going to sit down on the bench, next to the water pump. . . .

. . . The camcorder is going to linger over each of the graves, over each inscription, over each tombstone, and then a voice off-camera will speak of those men and those women, of the pogroms, of Czar Nicholas II, and after making a sweep, I'm going to open onto the port of Buenos Aires: the arrival of the immigrants, and I'll follow a man to wherever he's going . . . and zoom in on the train station . . . and zoom over an awning, and then on the farmers, the plague of locusts, and closing the diaphragm, I'll open with the story of Eichelbaum, *The Motionless Traveler*, the voice off-camera. After the flashback, a woman from Bobe's generation will speak about her life, and then I want to show a series of photos of Mama, as background to the story.

The driver tells me we're almost there, and that the cemetery's open until noon.

I want to bring to light those two years when Mama was so sick, and I want to see myself walking along the platform of the train station. I want Mama, Papa, and Bobe to ride with me in a taxi, like the one I'm in now, and I want Papa to talk to the driver about Fangio's kidnapping, and Mama and Bobe to talk about Aunt Berta, and I want to hear Papa say, "We're going to be late," and I want to be ten years old.

Then I want them to speak about everything they need to say, for as long as it takes to say what they couldn't tell me back then.

When I get out of the taxi, a man asks me, "Who are you looking for?"

"I'm looking for the tomb of Lete Resler."

The man gestures for me to follow him.

Fallow fields. Mist. Silence.

THE ARREST

TO ADY

It's hiding things makes them putrefy.
—*John Dos Passos*

One must imagine Sisyphus happy.
—*Albert Camus*

1
IN THE RICE FIELD

Vasili and Ana Finz came to Villa Clara with the immigrants brought over by Baron Hirsch, at the end of the nineteenth century. Finz taught himself the trade of rice farming, and started out as an *aguador*, maintaining the water level in the rice field.

After giving birth to Lucien, Ana died of eclampsia. A wet nurse breast-fed the child until his first birthday, and later, Finz's other sons took care of him. Finz leased seven acres with an adobe house and a barn. The boy grew up in the rice field, with the self-confidence his father, and especially his older brother Max, had instilled in him.

When Lucien could not fall asleep, Max would describe the thistle plants that flaunted their purple flowers at that hour, and he would tell him about the levees where the rice grew, and the minnows in the stream. And he would hum a Cossack song, nodding his head, "*Ayaya, yaya, yayaya.* . . ." Lucien would look up at the moonless sky and imagine his mother was somewhere in that darkness. Max would also tell him the story of the emperor who strutted around naked, convinced he was sporting a dashing suit, and a deep calm would come over the boy, lulling him to sleep.

Lucien's arms became strong from working the land.

"Lucien, turn that dirt over until it's light and airy," his father used to tell him.

The Finzes would take cover from the sun under the shade of a eucalyptus tree, and eat a frugal lunch, stretched out on the grass. After a short nap, they would go back to work. At sunset, they would eat heartily, drinking just one glass of wine, while they spoke about trivial matters. Then it was time to retire. Lucien preferred to take a walk before allowing sleep to overcome him.

In the summer, Vasili's forceful voice could be heard calling his sons and warning them, "An army of caterpillars is on the way. Find González to cast a spell on them."

The rice matured quickly, and the boy's shouts could be heard calling his father and brothers to see it flowering: "Noé, Max, come see the blossoms!"

When the harvest was good, the rice farmers from the neighboring villages would gather at the Finz house. A troupe of musicians with accordions and drums would strike up the initial strains of the *kazachok*. Max was always the first to stand in the middle of that ring of boys, and with his chest bare and arms extended he would leap suddenly and begin the dance, squatting and pounding the floor with the heels of his boots. Then he would spin in the air, dropping once again to his heels, as he continued dancing with grace and ease.

Respectable old men, Russian Jews, would surrender to the Cossack dance with powerful steps, singing, "*Yaya yayaya*," as if carried away by an unrepeatable pleasure.

Lucien took it all in, filling his head with sounds.

It had been raining for a week, the roads were flooded, and Malo Creek was running over; not even the horses could cross to the other shore. Lucien held his father's hand as he walked beside him. He could not have been more than eleven years old.

"Listen to the *pampero*, Lucien," you said, with your head bowed, wanting me to hear the early whispers of the southwesterly wind.

Vasili gazed out at the rice field.

"Is it going to clear up, Father?" I asked, and you told me that it would.

The rice field was a marsh, and the water came up to our knees. A rotten log and a coiled *yarará* snake drifted past my eyes.

A dead rat and a large storm cloud floated by as the water rushed furiously over the levees.

Vasili, you said you stayed up all night watching the rain fall, and you said that you'd risen from ruin more than once. But there were many things you didn't say. . . .

The army of caterpillars devoured the grain in a matter of hours, and the rain destroyed everything, but the Finzes were not the kind of people to surrender without a fight.

"We're leaving tomorrow, so get everything ready."

"But where are we going?" Max asked.

"To rent the land they offered me in Carlos Casares. We'll try to grow wheat."

"Carlos Casares is flooded too," Noé said.

"You're not willing to make sacrifices," Vasili said with a raspy voice, glaring at Noé.

Lucien remembered that his father's word was sacred.

I see you again, Father, walking slowly along the edge of the levee, deep in thought, sheltered by the silence. "The harvest is ruined," you say. The sun has gone into hiding and the muddy rice field smells like vomit. The air is still as twilight falls calmly. I hear the squawking of a scissor-tailed flycatcher soaring above, and the buzzing of electric-blue dragonflies darting all around. I see that the sky is pitch black in the distance, and I hear the dogs howling, and you, Father, murmuring, "But what more can I do?"

For more than three hours we trudged through the flooded rice field.

"How high is the water on the rod?" you asked Max.

"Damn, it's still rising!" he said.

"Don't speak like that, have you no decency?"

Max screamed back, "You think I'm still that boy who you forced to lie down under the sun, on a hot tin roof, because he refused to obey you. Humiliation and suffering, that's all that matters to you!"

"That's enough! Tell me my sacrifices were not in vain." Vasili said as he walked away from the rice field.

The screech of an owl disturbed the afternoon calm. I looked up at the sky and felt afraid: everything looked red, blood red.

"Let's rest now and come back when the water recedes," Noé said.

"Where's Lucien?" Max asked.

I was just a boy, but I'd heard everything and had gone off without saying a word. I only looked back when I felt Max's arms wrapping themselves around me.

"Hey, Lucien, take a deep breath, swallow the wind, and climb onto my shoulders. I'm going to give you a piggyback ride!"

And I got up on his shoulders, and we went galloping back to the house.

"Look over there, Lucien, that's where the Messiah's going to come, bringing peace and justice," you said. And because I was a God-fearing boy, I believed I saw him coming, mounted on his white horse. His thin face and long beard disappeared as soon as I opened my eyes. I couldn't fall back to sleep, Father.

Lucien was walking through the rice field when he heard someone singing a ballad in his grandparents' tongue, and he took it as a warning: "*I travel by sleigh / over the snowy steppe / with the wolves treading on my heels. . . .*"

The ground trembled, echoing in his ears. He heard a hushed murmur and quickened his pace. The storm would surely destroy the seed bed. When he got home, he heard the wind begin to shake the trees violently. Max had not returned, and they had to wait for the storm and the rain to end in order to look for him. They found him in the rice field, lifeless, his body burned and covered in mud, struck by a bolt of lightning. They carried him in their arms to the house.

"Put him on the sofa with his head at this end. We need to take off his shirt, his chest is burned," Vasili said, but he soon realized Max was dead, and threw himself, sobbing, over his body. Lucien could not breathe, and Noé only managed to let out a few faltering sounds.

They closed the casket and draped it with a black cloth that had a Star of David in the center, and placed it in the dining room for the wake. Speechless and unable to cry, Lucien clung to the coffin until Vera, Noé's wife, took him by the hand and led him away.

The farmers, dressed in deep mourning, stood together in the doorway of the Finz house, their rough faces filled with disbelief, speaking of Max as if he were alive. An old, robust woman burst into the wake, making her way through the crowd. She said she had been the boy's sixth grade teacher. When she saw the casket, a soft cry escaped her throat. She looked at a farmer by her side, and told him that as a boy Max had been good at numbers, and then she left.

They buried him in the town cemetery, according to the Law of Moses. Vasili prayed fervently at his son's grave, and called out his father's name, his voice laden with sorrow. Lucien stood there, looking at the cypresses: the shadow of their branches trembled on the ground. He watched a caterpillar crawl out of a grave, and thought that even in that place worms became masters of the dead.

Vera

In the afternoon, Noé's wife came in with a mug of hot milk and some poppy-seed buns and told him, "Eat! You haven't eaten all day, Lucien."

Lucien stared at the cleavage peeking out of her dress, and took a bite of a bun. Vera moved closer to him and caressed his head. His eyes were feverish, and he tried to control himself, but her hands led his toward her low neckline, and Lucien touched the breasts of that woman who almost could have been his mother.

During supper, Lucien laughed at everything.

"What's wrong with you?" Vasili asked him.

"Nothing . . . nothing . . ."

Lucien said that as soon as he finished high school, he would study medicine in Buenos Aires. Vasili assured him that his brother Boris would help him, and added that he was not going to let Lucien waste his life away in a village, "in this damn rice field full of caterpillars."

You turned fifty a long time ago, Father, and all of us at home believed you had feelings for a certain woman, even though you denied it. You didn't want to admit that a man who had loved my mother could love another woman.

Vera tells Lucien that Noé is never home. "He runs away from the house and works all day in the rice field."

Bewildered, Lucien remarks, "All of Villa Clara's talking about us, except Noé."

Lucien wants to forget that body. Closing his eyes, he can barely reconstruct Vera's face, her breasts, fading now in his memory.

I dreamed that Noé and I went out to look for Max with lightning striking all around, illuminating the rice field, and I thought I saw my mother standing amid the rice blossoms. Her skirt swirled in the wind, and I ran toward her, confused, and held her to my chest. Her hair brushed my face and neck, and a sensual, lingering scent rose from her body. Suddenly, I found myself looking straight into Noé's eyes, riveted on my face, and when I realized that woman was Vera, I couldn't breathe.

When I came to my senses, I remembered that widow who used to write love letters to you, Father. What was that woman's name? I found one of her letters: Matilde was her name . . . and you asked her to be so kind as to not write you anymore. I look at the sheet of paper once more, and see her name signed with a flourish I'll never forget.

I can see you now, Vasili, standing by the window, incapable of pronouncing a single word. You put a sunflower seed in your mouth, and the only sound is you spitting the shell onto the floor.

"Father, why don't you get married again?" I ask you.

"Me? . . . I'm an old man!" and you laugh like I rarely saw you laugh before.

Vera and Lucien lie naked on the straw. Vera kisses him and says she is going to eat him, and laughs. A few minutes earlier, Lucien had moaned with pleasure, and now he closes his eyes and feels only the turbulent flow of blood throbbing in his head, and he no longer knows if he is asleep or awake. A shape moves behind his eyes and vanishes in the darkness as Lucien turns his head and opens his eyes.

Vera draws him closer to her in the bed of straw, wanting him to make love to her again, but Lucien becomes tense and tells her, "We have to talk." Vera slips from his side and gets dressed, and Lucien puts on his pants. At that moment he hears Noé calling Vera, who goes out to meet him.

"Is something wrong?"

"I was looking for you."

Noé sees Lucien in the doorway of the barn and turns pale, then yells at him to go study and not waste time like some rich boy.

Lucien murmurs, "He knows. . . ."

Noé asks Lucien if he has seen Vera, and he answers no. Vasili has not come home yet, and the brothers sit down to eat, facing each other. Lucien does not speak. One look at Noé is enough to realize what is going on inside him. The silence is unbearable, and Lucien chuckles with a forced, awkward laugh that says it all.

Noé tells him, "Stop laughing and say what's on your mind, if you don't want me to smash your face. Where's Vera?"

Vera walks in, anxious, trying to appear calm as she thinks of something to say that will somehow save her. "Raquel kept me. . . . I'll bring the food right away, I just have to warm it."

She leaves her coat on a chair and crosses the dining room, her pleated skirt rustling softly as she walks. Vera has an innocent look on her face. Her dark hair falls onto her shoulders. Lucien does not look at her. Vera hurries into the kitchen, and when she returns with supper, she looks right through Lucien.

Noé asks, "Do we have any more *grapa*?"

Lucien rises from his seat and gets a half-filled bottle of grapa, and starts to serve Noé, but he grabs the bottle from Lucien and takes a swig, casting his desperate eyes from side to side. Lucien meets his gaze and feels a devastating chill.

Noé tells him about a farmer who has drowned, but it is not the same Noé who speaks. He seems strange, and says that the boat trip down the Uruguay River was too dangerous, and that the river was high. Lucien imagines himself at the train station, about to leave for Buenos Aires.

At that moment, Vasili comes in, excuses himself for being late for supper, and collapses into a chair, saying, "I finally paid the workers their wages, and they'll go back to Corrientes today. The harvest has been good. Let's toast to the harvest."

And Noé fills the glasses, and they raise them.

Lucien drinks one, two, then three glasses, his head throbs, and he drowses off. A memory races through his mind. The wind blows furiously and a eucalyptus branch rattles his bedroom window. It is nighttime. He is a nine-year-old boy, and from his bed, he looks through the window and sees the boogeyman threatening him, "When you come out, I'm going to take you away with me. . . ."

"No, I'm not leaving, I'm staying here," he thinks.

The boogeyman vanishes. Startled, Lucien sees Vasili, Vera, and Noé before him. He gets up from the table and goes outside. He vomits by the lilies, then breathes the fresh air and looks at the Southern Cross clinging to that sky. Lucien does not leave that spot until dawn breaks.

The next morning, the Finzes drink milk with bread and cheese before going to the rice field. Vasili asks Lucien what is bothering him.

"Nothing's wrong with him," Noé says.

Lucien answers that he cannot wait to go to Buenos Aires. Then Vasili reminds him that he has to speak with Mister Care, and dips his bread in the milk, and with his mouth full says that Alfredo Antik is going to marry a *goy*. Vasili looks at Lucien warily and exclaims, "It's unbelievable!"

Noé says it does not surprise him that things like that happen in Villa Clara, declaring that there are gentiles with no scruples, just as there are disgusting Jews who sleep with the wives of their friends.

Vasili loses his temper and forbids Noé from saying "such things" in front of Vera, then yanks the napkin from his collar and leaves.

"You better keep your mouth shut," Noé says.

Lucien does not say a word. Vera leaves the table and goes into the kitchen. Noé hands a book to Lucien and he reads:

> I. *Books and whores can be taken to bed.*
> II. *Books and whores are good for passing time. They*
> *rule night and day, and day and night.*
> III. *Books and whores: no one understands that for*
> *them, minutes are precious.*

Lucien trembles as he reads, with a shudder perceptible only to himself.

Vera enters the dining room with a stew, and when Noé tastes it, he says, "This meat smells like shit!" And he pounds his fist on the table and stands up, with his eyes piercing Vera's body.

She barely says a word, and Noé becomes furious again. Vera says timidly, "I'm sorry, I didn't mean to upset you."

"It's not her fault," Lucien says.

"You stay out of it, damn it!" Noé snarls. "And you, whore, get out of here!"

Silence. The door opens. Vasili enters and tells Vera the men need to talk about work, and asks her to leave them alone. It is the first time he shows hostility toward her. Vasili serves the rice pudding. Lucien does not eat, and Noé, his head bowed, rubs his inflamed eyes.

A cricket comes through the window and lands on Lucien's shirt, then rests on the floor, barely moving its antennae before suddenly taking flight.

"What do you want to talk about, Father?" Lucien asks.

Vasili says he can no longer remember.

The sun disappears behind the house. The moon is a white

horn. Lucien cannot utter a single word because there are no words to express what he is feeling.

We nod off, sitting on the straw. Max throws coins at my hat, startling me, and gets up and runs away with his hands tied behind his back, and I catch him, and he begs me to set him free.

Stretched out on the dining room sofa, Lucien asks himself again what he can do to forget Vera. He spends the entire afternoon on that sofa, staring through the beige curtains. Lucien remembers the night his father raised his glass and toasted, "To Vera, the most beautiful girl in Colonia Clara." And he toasted her as well. And so did Noé, vigorous like a happy animal.

But Vera has a scent that excites him, and she knows it, and Lucien feels it in his body and in his insomnia.

Lucien paces nervously. He hears only the voices of the reapers and the whisper of the rice sheaves falling to the ground. He goes to the cemetery to visit Max's tomb, and opens the siddur and reads:

זְמוֹר שִׁיר חֲנֻכַּת הַבַּיִת לְדָוִד. אֲרוֹמִמְךָ, יְיָ, כִּי דִלִּיתָנִי,
שִׂמַּחְתָּ אֹיְבַי לִי. יְיָ אֱלֹהָי, שִׁוַּעְתִּי אֵלֶיךָ וַתִּרְפָּאֵנִי. יְיָ,
יתָ מִן שְׁאוֹל נַפְשִׁי, חִיִּיתַנִי מִיָּרְדִי בוֹר. זַמְּרוּ לַיְיָ חֲסִידָיו,
וּ לְזֵכֶר קָדְשׁוֹ. כִּי רֶגַע בְּאַפּוֹ, חַיִּים בִּרְצוֹנוֹ; בָּעֶרֶב יָלִין
, וְלַבֹּקֶר רִנָּה. וַאֲנִי אָמַרְתִּי בְשַׁלְוִי, בַּל אֶמּוֹט לְעוֹלָם. יְיָ,
וֹנְךָ הֶעֱמַדְתָּה לְהַרְרִי עֹז; הִסְתַּרְתָּ פָנֶיךָ, הָיִיתִי נִבְהָל.
ד יְיָ אֶקְרָא, וְאֶל אֲדֹנָי אֶתְחַנָּן. מַה בֶּצַע בְּדָמִי, בְּרִדְתִּי
שָׁחַת; הֲיוֹדְךָ עָפָר, הֲיַגִּיד אֲמִתֶּךָ. שְׁמַע יְיָ וְחָנֵּנִי; יְיָ, הֱיֵה
לִי. הָפַכְתָּ מִסְפְּדִי לְמָחוֹל לִי; פִּתַּחְתָּ שַׂקִּי וַתְּאַזְּרֵנִי
וה. לְמַעַן יְזַמֶּרְךָ כָבוֹד, וְלֹא יִדֹּם; יְיָ אֱלֹהָי, לְעוֹלָם
דֶ.

תְּגַּדַּל וְיִתְקַדַּשׁ שְׁמֵהּ רַבָּא בְּעָלְמָא דִי בְרָא כִרְעוּתֵהּ;
יךְ מַלְכוּתֵהּ בְּחַיֵּיכוֹן וּבְיוֹמֵיכוֹן, וּבְחַיֵּי דְכָל בֵּית יִשְׂרָאֵל,
לָא וּבִזְמַן קָרִיב, וְאִמְרוּ אָמֵן.
הֵא שְׁמֵהּ רַבָּא מְבָרַךְ לְעָלַם וּלְעָלְמֵי עָלְמַיָּא.
תְּבָרַךְ וְיִשְׁתַּבַּח, וְיִתְפָּאַר וְיִתְרוֹמַם, וְיִתְנַשֵּׂא וְיִתְהַדָּר,
לֶּה וְיִתְהַלָּל שְׁמֵהּ דְּקֻדְשָׁא, בְּרִיךְ הוּא, לְעֵלָּא (לְעֵלָּא)
ל בִּרְכָתָא וְשִׁירָתָא, תֻּשְׁבְּחָתָא וְנֶחֱמָתָא, דַּאֲמִירָן בְּעָלְמָא,
דּוּ אָמֵן.
הֵא שְׁלָמָא רַבָּא מִן שְׁמַיָּא, וְחַיִּים, עָלֵינוּ וְעַל כָּל יִשְׂרָאֵל,
רוּ אָמֵן.
נֶשֶׂה שָׁלוֹם בִּמְרוֹמָיו, הוּא יַעֲשֶׂה שָׁלוֹם עָלֵינוּ וְעַל כָּל
אֵל, וְאִמְרוּ אָמֵן.

Then he closes the prayer book. The parakeets chatter in the palm trees, announcing a storm. Lucien sits on a rock, his eyes pursuing a hummingbird as it sucks a Persian buttercup. The hummingbird flies away as if swept by the wind.

Vasili took out a glass rimmed with a Grecian border, and wiped it carefully with his shirttail. He served some buttered toast to Noé, who rubbed his bloodshot eyes and did not speak.

Outside, the wind cut like a knife, and the frost burned the rice field.

Vasili says, "Pain also passes, Noé," and stares into the emptiness as if he were thinking that this son would also leave, and that it was only a matter of time before the door would close for the last time.

"Your tea's getting cold," Vasili tells him.

And the two lonely men lean over the table and drink their tea in silence.

You say there's no land as generous as this one. Why do you idealize everything, Father? Perhaps it's because you've lost touch with the ground under your feet. We forget that we're not yet inhabitants of this country, just squatters.

When Mister Care learned that Lucien was going to Buenos Aires, he gave him a letter of recommendation to give a man named Malgarejo, who would hire him. Mister Care was in charge of the General Urquiza Railway, and knew the Finzes.

"When you tell him that I'm sending you, Malgarejo will not turn you away," said the Englishman as he buttoned his topcoat.

"I'll write you, Father," Lucien said, and Vasili bid his son farewell, bestowing his blessings upon him.

It was Sunday, and Lucien wandered around the port for a while. He watched a passenger ship with an Italian flag, which was docked at one of the piers.

Max's voice still resounds in his ears, telling him, "The irrigation ditches are ready. . . ."

And he believes he still hears his father's voice: "The rice field needs to be covered with water, two inches, in November and December. . . ."

He hears the murmur of the creek, the shrill squawking of the wild ducks, and their wings fluttering over the glassy water.

Father, you said you came with Mama on the *Wesser*, and that her last name was Yagupsky. And you said *Yagu* is a tree that grows on the Russian steppe and attracts lightning, and that *sky* means "son of."

Max was struck dead by a lightning bolt, and I believed he had died because he was the son of that tree, which was my mother, and I thought that I could die that way too. . . . But I like storms.

Noé said that Mama was always bent over a tub, scrubbing clothes, and afterward she would dry her hands on her apron and read some pages that she had written. Noé also said that one day those sheets flew away like scissor-tailed flycatchers, and followed you, with some other birds, behind the plow you pushed.

Sitting in his room on Azcuénaga Street, with pen in hand, Lucien sees himself once again plunging a shovel into the muddy soil and lifting it out, full of caterpillars.

"The water's running over and we're going to lose everything."

The air smells like mud. The green army advances across the rice field like a regiment that devastates an entire region, ravaging it.

"That damn army of caterpillars isn't going to leave us a thing!"

A few lapwings carry away some of those worms in their beaks. The caterpillars leave behind a heap of dead shoots.

I imagine you leaning against the trunk of a eucalyptus tree, your tense face vigilant, your own solitude blending into the silence of the ridge. I can still hear you saying that Jewish farmers know nothing more than plows and books, books and plows, that's what you say over and over, as if you were still under the watchful eye of the Cossacks.

Boris Finz fixed up a room for his nephew in his apartment on Azcuénaga Street. Boris lived alone in an apartment in the *Once* neighborhood. He was sixty-five years old, and looked like his brother Vasili, with his thin build, fair skin, long slender fingers, and the light-blue eyes of a Slavic Jew. He was a prudent man, but at the same time, unpredictable. He worked for the Graphic Arts Union as an editor for *La Protesta*, and had a little savings.

Lucien began to read everything his uncle gave him. He liked mystery stories, and had just read *The Murders in the Rue Morgue*.

"Mister Care's letter of recommendation was just what I needed. I'm working as a clerk for the railway, and have the afternoons and evenings to study. Señor Malgarejo is a good man, and we get along well, but I'm finding it hard to get used to Buenos Aires.

"I like to walk into the bars on a street called Triunvirato, order a cup of coffee, and watch the people talking about things that don't concern me. I feel as if I'm wearing a watch that hasn't been wound. Time stands still in the country, while in Buenos Aires everything happens too quickly.

"There are many people who humiliate or hurt you, when they realize you're not like them. I thought about how you warned me, Father, to be careful with city folk.

"Uncle Boris put me up in his apartment, but he said he wouldn't be able to keep me very long. I realize he can barely make ends meet. I'm going to pay him back every last cent I owe him, I promise you."

I dreamed I saw Max, and he asked me if it was true that I had returned to Villa Clara just so he could insult me. Then Max called over a husky man standing behind me, and told him to take me away. I wondered in my sleep who that man could be. The man laughed and repeated to me, "Jew, Jew," until finally I woke up.

Lucien went out for a walk. It had started to rain. He stayed clear of dark areas, and went down Triunvirato, crossing in front of a hotel. The sound of a typewriter could be heard through the open door of the entrance. On Canning Street, he saw an open bar and went in. It was full of people, and Lucien ordered a cup of coffee at the bar. He looked at his watch: it was a quarter past two. Lucien's eyes fell on a buxom woman with a cherubic face and curly hair, wearing a tight dress. She had bright red lips and smelled of cheap perfume. The woman went over to Lucien and asked him, "So are you a country boy?" She spoke in a hoarse voice, like someone used to night life. The woman told Lucien she liked him, and whispered in his ear that she would not charge him much.

Lucien looked at the woman again, and a shiver ran through his body. Her long legs reminded him of Vera's. The woman took him by the arm, and they went out to the street, and crossed it. Then Lucien found himself in a hallway and heard the sound of a key turning in the lock of a door. Suddenly, he saw himself in a room with a large bed, separated from a privy by a dirty muslin curtain.

"You want a beer?" the woman asked as she began to undress. Lucien looked at her without speaking, but the woman he saw was not the one he wanted to see. She sat on his lap and caressed his face, then slid her fingers down his chest, but when she tried to slip her hand into his pants, he stopped her. She said, "Don't be silly, take off your pants." And she waited for him, stretched out on the bed. Lucien hesitated.

"Come here."

Lucien ran his hands over her thighs, and then stepped back.

"You're the first man who doesn't want to grope me."

A minute later, Lucien walked out of the room, leaving her some money on the nightstand. He headed for Gurruchaga Street. The fresh air hit him in the face and made him feel better. He remembered that hot February afternoon when he was riding a horse and fell to the ground, then lay there until Vera came. He looked into her eyes and she told him the wound was not deep. She was wearing a navy-blue dress, and Lucien glimpsed her skin beneath the slip, her dark nipples under the lace, and he leaned his head against her breasts, without speaking, and heard the beating of her heart, like the trickle of water running over the rice field.

That was after Ernesto Banchik told Lucien that Vera was deceiving Noé, but he refused to tell him with whom. Lucien knew Ernesto well: he was a man of few words.

Lucien remembers waiting for her in his room. When he saw her come in wearing a pale, short-sleeved dress, he ran over and kissed her on the mouth, and told her if she were his wife, he would make her wear long sleeves like a *bobe*. Vera laughed, and Lucien slid his hand down her neck, pressed her against his body, and kissed her passionately on the neck, and then said to her, "I know you have another lover."

Vera told him to stop talking nonsense.

Lucien opened the door, and told her, "Leave."

Vera was going to say something, but Lucien told her again, "Leave." She walked out, and Lucien felt like a child burning with rage.

I remembered it was Friday, and I thought you were probably in the temple reciting the Prayer of the Dead. The trunk was so heavy, my whole body ached. I stopped along the road and watched the afternoon fall over the rice field. Then I continued on to the train station.

The waiting room was barely illuminated by a kerosene lamp. Some farmers shook hands, welcoming the new year. Among them was a rice farmer, one of his father's friends, but when Lucien went over to greet him, the man turned his back on him.

    Lucien left the room and found a spot on the platform to wait.

Ernesto Banchik told me that Vera was sleeping with Marcos Barg, and that he'd seen them in the hay field. The afternoon that Vera left the house was the afternoon I also saw her with Marcos Barg, near Malo Creek, on my way back from Basavilbaso.

    The train pulled out of the Villa Clara station and the rice field passed before his eyes. Winding turns and the persistent stench of rotten slime. The train entered a tunnel, and everything turned dark. He pressed his face against the window and sank down into his seat. And once again, he saw the green fields and the black dirt drifting past his eyes like a shadow over his face. The clattering of the train and the sound of the wagon coupler confused him. He thought he heard the creaking of a brass bed, and suddenly he saw Marcos Barg's hands touching Vera's naked body, and Lucien approached slowly, and when he was one step from Marcos Barg, he confessed his love for Vera to him. And Marcos proposed, with an air of generosity that Lucien did not believe he deserved, that if they both loved her so much, all three of them should live together. At that moment, the guard asked for his ticket, and Lucien opened his eyes and thought that dreams are always an intolerable lie.

Lucien observed the telephone lines rising and falling against a background of thick clouds. He walked from one end of the coach to the other, crossed the coupler, and meandered restlessly through the cars. He returned to his seat and began to read a magazine.

He walked down Canning, dodging trucks and cars. The noise of each passing car made him nervous.

It was the first time Lucien had ever ridden a trolley and he was afraid it would jump the track. He found himself thinking about Vera again, but it made no sense to remember his brother's wife. It was not easy to keep his resolve to not think about her. Through the window, he watched Buenos Aires pass by at high speed before his eyes, and he counted the minutes left until he would arrive at the railway office. When he got off, he thought it would be hard to get used to that whirlwind pace.

At the School of Medicine, he met a fellow with a foreign accent. They spoke for a while and agreed to study together. He told Lucien his name was Luigi Melle and that he worked in the slaughterhouse. He spoke about his boss, as if Lucien knew him, "He said I was a lousy Italian, and he wasn't going to pay me a cent."

Luigi Melle, his eyes fixed on Lucien's face, went on to say, "*Dio cane* . . . ! If I'm a lousy Italian, he's a miserable Dutchman."

He paused and declared, "When the revolution comes, no one's going to work for anyone else, and it'll be like waking from a dream. That's what Enrico Malatesta said. . . . *Dio cane*. . . . Everything started with the Commune. . . ."

Whenever they got together, Luigi Melle spoke to him about the need to change society, and Lucien listened to him, but was afraid to get involved with anything but his studies.

"I don't get involved in politics," he told him, his face tense, trying to appear confident. Luigi Melle told Lucien before leaving, "We'll talk some other day. . . ."

His Uncle Boris had given him some pamphlets from the Graphic Arts Union to distribute among his fellow workers at the railway office. When he got off the trolley, he ran into an agent, who asked to see his permit for distributing them. Lucien did not know what to say and ran away, throwing the pamphlets into a garbage bin.

Lucien put Gley's *Physiology* on the table, and before settling down to study, looked out the window at the dark night, and as if he were seeing his childhood, the image of his favorite hiding place in his house came rushing back to him.

I'm hiding behind the drapes and I become a white shape that moves cautiously. I can't be more than nine years old, and I hear my father, Max, and Noé come in the house, and I hide under the dining room table. They don't suspect I'm under the table, or that's what I believe, and I surprise them with a shriek, and they freeze in place. And I probably tell them that they're under arrest and that they must obey, and I make them repeat after me: *AVE CAESAR IMPERATOR, MORITURI TE SALUTANT,* and after they repeat Caesar's words, I release them.

Boris Finz organized political meetings in his house with his comrades from the Graphic Arts Union. Lucien would hear them speak about solidarity and creating a common front among the working class. And they would applaud, "To better wages, to the revolution!"

Lucien refused to take part in the discussions with his uncle and his friends.

"The call for a general strike must put an end to the political massacres. And the Vasena factory . . ."

Those voices disturbed Lucien. How could he possibly concentrate on his studies with all that uproar and commotion? He left and walked down Triunvirato, with nowhere in particular to go. He stopped under an awning to light a cigarette, and stood there, contemplating the water as it flowed into a drain. The city lights went out, and when they came back on, he thought he saw Noé's face, but it disappeared instantly.

As the drizzle fell on the sidewalk, the sound of an approaching trolley shook him out of his thoughts. After boarding, he saw that his next-door neighbor was in the seat facing him. She was a redhead, perhaps in her forties. Lucien stared at the purple marks on her neck, but neither the marks nor the wrinkles around her eyes diminished her beauty. The woman crossed her long legs, and he noticed her silk stockings. Lucien stared at her intently the whole way, then shivered when she returned his gaze.

For several days they crossed paths on the stairs and spoke to each other. The redhead told him that she was going to be late for work, and that she was a cashier, without mentioning where she worked.

"My name is Amalia," she said.

It was the last time he saw her. The redhead's body was like a painful memory that only vanished from his thoughts with the routine of work.

Né Dio né Padrone

He put on the hat his father had given him, and walked to a kiosk to buy a newspaper. He turned to the classified ads and read, "Room for rent to a responsible student." Lucien had not yet told his Uncle Boris that he would be moving out. Before doing so, he needed to find a room somewhere. The following day he would go to the boarding house Luigi Melle had recommended to him.

Lucien walked to the waterfront and stayed there for a long time, gazing at the stormy, turbulent river as it pounded the dock. Then he decided to return.

No one was home in the apartment on Azcuénaga Street. It was three in the morning, and he went into his room and washed out a shirt and pair of pants. He hung the clothes in the window of his room. Then he opened Testut's *Anatomy*, but could not concentrate on his reading. He peered out his window and saw light in the redhead's bedroom, and the silhouette of a fat man outlined in the window.

Uncle Boris had mentioned in passing that the redhead next door had a drunk husband. Perhaps that hefty shadow framed in the window belonged to her husband. The man moved his arms and gestured as if threatening someone. Lucien closed the shutters and went to bed. Uncle Boris had not yet returned from *La Protesta*.

It rained hard all night, and thunder rattled the window pane, keeping Lucien awake. Off and on he heard the ringing of the trolley bell fading into a dull murmur: near, far, near, far. . . .

Lucien boarded the trolley, taking off his hat before sitting down. He wanted to find the boarding house his friend Luigi had recommended. He raised the small window and a blast of hot air hit him in the face. The street was deserted and the heat and humidity rose like a thick cloud over the cobblestones.

Everything happened that sultry week in January, Father.

Suddenly, Lucien heard a terrible noise, followed by loud gunshots, and he jumped off the trolley. Someone told him a bomb had exploded in Nueva Pompeya and another one in the Jewish neighborhood. He was stunned, and remembered Vasili telling him about how his father and mother had been murdered in a pogrom by Cossacks, and he thought, "There can't be pogroms here. . . ."

You told me about the hardships they endured under Czar Nicholas II, and you cursed him and repeated that I should never forget that, if I didn't want that tragedy to happen again. I imagined Czar Nicholas with an arrogant face and a mouth filled with contempt, similar to the portrait of the landowner in my sixth grade reader.

Now I understand, Father, why you harped on me to study more than anyone else, saying, "If you want to be someone, Lucien, your education has to be the main reason for living. . . If you study, a man like the Czar will never be born in this country. . ."

A strong smell of gunpowder shook Lucien from his lethargy. He got off the trolley and heard voices. Disoriented, he crossed the street. He came upon a group of workers putting up a barricade and walked away from there. Lucien saw a car enveloped in flames. He was there, but he could not believe his eyes or ears. Men, women, and children were being dispersed by the police. He ran, dodging rocks and bullets. He heard the screams of the wounded who were lying on the ground. A man drenched in blood cried out for help. Lucien grabbed him by the arm, but the man shouted in pain, and he could not move him. Lucien told the man to be calm, that he was going to get help. He crossed the corner and saw a woman lying on the sidewalk, her mouth open as if she were shouting, but she was dead.

The people ran, confused and frightened, amid the rumble, and he ran too, aimlessly, afraid, like all the others. At that moment, he heard a voice from a megaphone urging people to leave the streets and return home. "Cooperate with the police. We will take rigorous measures to remove those who try to create chaos in the nation. . . ."

Lucien stopped in front of a store with a bolted door, and did not hesitate to force the padlock open and take refuge there. He was shaking, and had lost the hat his father had given him. His shirt clung to his body, and the only thing he could hear was his own breathing. His forehead was covered in cold sweat, and he loosened his tie and went down an iron staircase leading to the basement.

Lucien could not remember when he had jumped from the trolley.

You used to say, Father, "The lemongrass is invasive and takes over the rice. You have to pull it up by hand, one by one."

Max, Noé, and I pulled up the wild grass, one by one, until we were exhausted and out of breath after working for hours under the sun. Then you'd say, "How can my sons get so tired from doing nothing?" And you'd stand there, Father, looking out over the rice field, which seemed like a mirror in the evening light.

Later, Lucien heard someone opening the small window, then two policemen climbed into the basement, and without giving him a chance to explain what he was doing there, they handcuffed him and threw him to the floor. One of the uniformed men insulted him. The man had fierce eyes and an angular face. He screamed at him, "Russky!" and twisted his mouth as if he were chewing a lemon. The other policeman, whose right eye blinked constantly, shouted at him, "Hey, Catalan, we've been looking for you for some time now!"

And he began to swear, "Son of a bitch, striker, Russky!"

As long as I live I'll never forget his raised hand pointing a gun at me. He took away the gold watch that once belonged to Max, my money, and everything else I had in my pockets. One of the policemen punched me in the stomach. My mouth was dry and my head dizzy. I didn't have the strength to say a single word. He looked at me, Father, the way you said they looked at you when you came to Buenos Aires.

I was born at the wrong time. I have to struggle even though my life remains hard and agonizing. I feel as if I've been riding a horse on a long journey, ever since I was born. Buenos Aires can't force me to give up my dignity.

When the creek rises it's treacherous, but when you measure the water with a stick and keep an eye on the rising water, you know you can divert it with the pump and send it to higher ground. I'm going to put up a fight, Father.

I couldn't have been more than eight years old, and I remember telling you that I'd seen a white owl with a rat in its mouth. And I told you when the mice crushed the grains with their teeth, and you reassured me that the bats would take care of the mice.

They took Lucien to police headquarters, where hundreds of people were being detained. They kept him out in the rain until dusk. A guard kept watch with a rifle across his chest.

They recorded his personal information, took his fingerprints, and ordered him to wait. He told them his arrest was a mistake, but they did not listen to him.

A German shepherd slept at the feet of the policeman guarding him. He told Lucien that if the dog woke up and tried to bite him, it was a sign he was a Russian anarchist. The dog opened his eyes, barked ferociously, and lunged at him.

"Dogs are never wrong," the policeman said, and Lucien remembered that when the dogs barked at dawn in Villa Clara, it was a bad omen.

Somewhere near police headquarters a tango could be heard playing on a radio.

Lucien hears footsteps coming down the hall, footsteps of a man dragging himself, exhausted. A specter passes by slowly and looks at him, with his hands cuffed, a being that a few days ago was called Luigi Melle. Lucien stares at him, searches for him, only to find hollow eyes, empty holes. He is hunched over. They stuck needles in his face and beat him brutally. The guard pushes him to make him walk faster, and screams at him, "Move it!"

Lucien realizes that in Buenos Aires there is no room for two ideas. The city is a stifling place, with its stagnant, asphyxiating air, closed behind an iron door.

He sat on a bench for a long time, until a stocky man in a linen suit and shiny shoes opened the door and motioned him into an office. The man was about forty years old. He wrote Lucien's name on a form, and the only sound was that of his pen scratching the paper.

"When they brought your file, I noticed your last name. What origin is it?" he said, pronouncing the name *Finz* in a harsh tone. He ordered Lucien to tell him about the anarchist plan against the country.

He turned on the fan, which was sitting on his desk, and put his face in front of it to get some air. Lucien repeated that they were wrong about him.

"Speak up, Finz. . . ."

A few bands of light filtered through the half-closed shutters.

Lucien tried to explain how they had captured him, but was abruptly interrupted. "How long have you been working for the cause? Speak, if you don't want things to get ugly."

Max was dead, and you, Vasili, would write him letters that you kept in a wooden box. I used to rummage through it, and I read a few letters you wrote to my dead brother. They sounded like a prayer. I learned from those letters that when Max was twelve years old, he still slept in bed with my mother. You used to say, Father, that she was a good woman from a well-to-do Kishinev family, and that she worried about everyone except herself. It seems she never got used to the harsh life of Villa Clara. Did it matter to you, Father, that your wife wasn't cut out for the life of a farmer? She raised Max and Noé, leaving behind part of herself. Even though I never knew her, I think about her now—perhaps I'm delirious, but I know there's something of my mother in me, I don't know what. . . . My ears believe they hear her whispering in the shadows of this filthy room, laden with dreams.

Ever since I came to Buenos Aires, I wanted to understand what was happening in the country, but I didn't really care about politics. I'm an employee of the railways, and I don't have time to participate in union meetings. Something tells me the government won't allow things to get out of hand.

"*Hey little bourgeois / time to tighten your belt / today the rich / are nearly ruined. / And your savings, / auto and mansion / will soon* *vanish / down a trapdoor. / Looks like the Commie rage / has made it this way / and is raring to go here. . . ."**

The man warned him that his name was on a blacklist. His eyes shone like fish scales, and he said, "Your father came from Russia, and was a boarder at the Immigrant Hotel in 1898. A lot of filthy, rowdy people stayed at that hotel."

Then he raised his voice. "And now, I have before me his son, a troublemaker who works for the railway, who resides in 'our boardinghouse,' since the dawn of January 8, 1919, and who is going to explain to me where his father got that name for him: Lucien. What a name for a farmer!"

The officer from the Civil Guard took out a revolver and placed it on the table, and while Lucien wiped the blood from his nose with a handkerchief, the man played with the trigger of the gun, making comments about Jews, anarchists, and Italians.

The officer let the gun fall to the tile floor, and it fired. Then he burst into laughter and looked at Lucien, saying, "So you're afraid of me, you fucking Russky. Don't give me that look, I'm all out of patience. I'm not asking you to tell me what girl you laid, and in what whorehouse, what I want is for you to do as I say, if you don't want to spend the rest of your life in the dark."

Then the man said in a serious tone, "Tell me about your friend Luigi Melle and the meetings at the Confitería París."

Lucien remained silent and remembered Luigi used to read a Russian poet:

"With those eyes of hers / you better take care / not to look at them / or you'll never forget them. . . ."

Then the officer told him, "Luigi Melle came from Italy two years ago and speaks Spanish fluently."

---

*Lyrics from a popular tango of that era.

Lucien admired the confident way in which Luigi expressed his ideas, while Luigi used to say he admired how Lucien valued what was real and lasting.

Lucien wondered if it had been he who was riding the trolley in search of the boarding house where Luigi lived, or someone else, when all this started that hot, muggy January morning.

And the man continued interrogating him, "Do you know that Luigi Melle broke into a gun shop? Do you know that fag murdered a friend of the Civil Guard? Your comrade believed in revolutionary strikes, or don't you remember he founded '*Né Dio né Padrone*'?"

"Luigi Melle is an anarchist," he said, and shook the straw hat lying on his desk. He lit a cigarette, drank his coffee, and then said, "As they say in Italy now, '*ci vuole bastone, bastone e bastone.*'

Lucien saw the fury in his eyes. The officer quickly changed his tone of voice, and asked him to tell him about his job in the railway office. And when he asked about the books Lucien had read, he remarked, "You're what they call an educated farmer. Tell me, what have you read by Rosa Luxemburg?"

Lucien remained calm and answered that he had never read anything by Rosa Luxemburg, and then the man told him, "Christ, I've never heard of a Bolshevik who hasn't read something by that woman." And he kicked him in the stomach, threatening him, "I'm going to cut off your balls."

Lucien could not stand, but the man forced him to get up, and he moaned.

"Would you look at who's complaining, the Jew who came from the country to the city to fight slavery."

Lucien said his accusation was false, but the man responded, "You read the entire works of that woman. We found among your possessions: *The Accumulation of Capital, The Mass Strike, the Political Party, and the Trade Unions*, and an issue of *Leipziger Volkszeitung*. Should I go on? Do you want to keep lying, Finz?"

The arm he had in a sling hurt, and he talked to himself. The guard ordered him to shut up. He thought he heard the crack of a whip and the pounding of heels, and he lay rigid in the cot and screamed, "Save me, Father!" The guard told him again to shut up, and when Lucien kept talking, he kicked him in the head with his thick-soled shoes, repeating, "If you want more, I can give you more. . . ."

Lucien was unconscious for a long time. When he came to, he heard them telling him, "You don't make it easy on us, you fucking Russky. . . ."

He remembered when the black rain fell in Villa Clara, and the sky was pierced by tongues of fire and thunder roared, and he thought he saw a shape moving behind his bedroom curtain. And now another shape was moving and speaking with other forms—perhaps they were the dead murmuring something before parting from the living.

"The only thing that'll cure him is prison," resounded the words of the officer in his ears.

"The bomb went off when he went to throw it. . . . Luigi Melle died before he got to the hospital."

And now the officer is saying to him, "You're not a farmer anymore, but you can't stop being one either."

In his stupor, he believed he was carrying the trunk his father brought with him from Kishinev, that he was in the port, and that Max was there too, hauling stalks of rice to a boat.

"Are the mulberries turning dark yet?"

And he heard Max telling him, "The rice field is in full bloom, and ever since father died, we need you. . . ."

How is it possible that he did not know his father had passed away? Lucien asked what had happened to their father, and Max told him that some Cossacks had murdered him.

You told me that when you were a boy you used to go fishing with my Grandfather Aczel. And you sold sardines along the Dnieper River all the way to the Vistula, even during snowstorms. You said the train stopped in Kishinev, and two Cossacks boarded. They were drunk and laughing. One of them spat on Grandfather Aczel, while the other one took out his saber and grabbed him by an ear. You also said that your father managed to tell you, "Vasili, run," and you scurried through the train cars and hid behind a trunk. You told me that you saw the Cossacks hurl my grandfather with one shove into the emptiness.

Lucien was very anxious and wanted to see the officer again.

"I want a lawyer," he told him.

The man responded that it would be better if Lucien told him about the political propaganda he had printed on the railway's mimeograph machine.

They want to send me to Ushuaia. Exile can last a lifetime. You know about the confusion, fear, and hatred they make you suffer. They hurt you and beat you like it's the most natural thing in the world. Last night they subjected me to what they call an "examination of conscience." They stuck my head in a bucket of water, and I don't know what happened to me next, but when I opened my eyes, I felt life coming back to me, in the form of pain.

I try to understand what's happening. Not understanding is terrible.

The history I learned in school said that barbarism is in the country, and civilization in the city. What happened here this week makes Buenos Aires seem like a sea of barbarism, a huge city where perverse customs may be seen, and an irritating murmur can be heard that makes a person feel like a foreigner in his own country. I want you to know I'm not going to confess to something I didn't do.

Those in command here unload their resentment toward life, and enjoy those acts they commit with unbridled fury. You never know what may happen to you, or what someone is capable of doing out of weakness, or whatever you want to call that blind emotion you feel when someone tries to destroy your will to live.

You taught me what is worthwhile in life, and I'm grateful to you for passing that legacy on to me. I want to be a doctor, and I'm not going to give up that dream, but I'm afraid to spend the rest of my life in prison in Tierra del Fuego.

Did nothing exist other than that voice telling me whatever it felt like saying, Father? What had I done for that man to punish me that way?

After taking a break from work, we ate some tortillas and rested under the shade of a magnolia tree. My father placed a bunch of hay under his neck, ran his hand over his bald head, and lay still, lost in his thoughts as if I were not there. Now it seems that I see in his harsh face the look of a boy threatened by hunger, darkness, and snow, a boy who wants to escape Kishinev.

I remember, Father, how you would look around and cast your eyes upon the rice field, and say to me, "What land this is, Lucien—whatever you plant grows!"

You said my mother was your only love, and surely your last happiness, and you tried to hide your feelings.

A *sirirí* duck flew by, quacking over our heads. My father followed it with his eyes, without saying a word.

The shots resounded beyond the walls of police headquarters. A policeman knocked on the office door, entered, and announced that the army had taken control of the city, and soldiers were shooting the anarchists in Balvanera, Villa Crespo, Barracas, and Nueva Pompeya, with sharpshooters positioned in Chacarita and Almagro. The policeman left after exchanging a few words with the officer from the Civil Guard, who then turned to Lucien and said he was in favor of a "reasonably patriotic" solution. He threw away his cigarette, and after a few minutes said, "They found Melle's body at the corner of Yatay and Triunvirato, with a bullet in the neck."

A shiver ran up and down Lucien's body. He could not breathe, as if his lungs were being crushed by a beam. The officer ordered Lucien, "Speak up; don't play games, Finz. You're too educated to be the simple farmer you pretend to be. You know, don't you, that you talk in your sleep?"

He opened a bottle of gin and began to drink, one glass after another, but remained sober. When his eyes became bloodshot from the alcohol, he told him, "I'm not going to leave you in peace, if you can't bring yourself to remember. . . . It's one in the morning and you're not going to keep me here all night. You don't have a record, Lucien. . . . Let's see, Simón. I need some information, Lucien. . . . I doubt your name is Simón. That's your alias, and it's no coincidence you were named after that convicted anarchist who came from Russia with your Uncle Boris, and on the very same boat, even. Don't look at me like you don't know I'm talking about Radovitzky. What a way to start the century, Simón!"

Lucien told him he didn't know what he was talking about.

"Let me explain. . . . It's not easy to bear the alias of that Russian, not easy at all. . . . And don't look at me like you just discovered gunpowder. It must be hard enough for you with that name your parents gave you."

And the officer showed him where to sign. Lucien told him that what was written there were vile, false accusations, and he refused to sign.

"You're a liar. I have here in my hands the report on the attack on the 26th District Precinct."

Lucien told him if he thought he was going to intimidate him with that, he was mistaken. Then the officer said, "I wonder what it's like to be a Jew. . . ."

We were on the patio, and you pulled a thorn from the bottom of my foot, and I told you that a man from Corrientes said the world would end soon, and you laughed and told me about Halley's Comet, which was streaking through the sky about that time.

Lucien heard a man panting like a blacksmith's bellows and screaming, "No!" Suddenly, a tango began to play on the radio, with the volume loud enough to muffle the cries of the gasping man.

"Get it in your head, what you don't decide to do yourself, will be decided for you. You could be sent to prison in Ushuaia."

And the officer read a page regarding a suspect who had approached the door of police headquarters screaming, "Long live anarchy!" as he attacked one of the agents. He read, "Immediately afterward, because the scoundrel resisted, one of our agents unloaded six bullets into his chest. The victim was identified as Luigi Melle."

"If it's true Luigi Melle's dead, as you say, it's because you killed him," I told him.

The officer said the "hunt for Russians" was underway, and that I couldn't understand the words of the national anthem, and he had an obligation to protect the welfare of the homeland.

"Tomorrow I want you to talk about your participation in the Córdoba rebellion, that's right . . . last year, with those bourgeois students. You're going to tell me all about that uprising that threatens the Nation."

Then the officer pointed his gun at me, put the barrel to my forehead, and fired three shots. When I finally opened my eyes, I heard him order a guard to take me away and keep an eye on me.

You used to say that whenever the wild ducks gave birth, the roots of the rice plants would move restlessly in the mud. You also said that in order for the rice blossoms to grow, someone had to admire them, and you'd keep them company for long periods of time.

Now I see a circle of light, and within that circle is the officer interrogating me, taking his time as he questions me. Whenever he says my name, he pronounces it with a French accent, then hits me again, and asks about Luigi Melle, and I cry, and he tells me not to be a sissy.

Once again Lucien sees that white shape who entered his bedroom window whenever he was afraid of a storm, and he remembers that he used to call him the Bat Man.

An agent told him to follow him. They went down a long corridor and entered a tiny room, and there another guard ordered him to strip. Lucien tried to resist, but the guard yanked down his pants, and screamed at him, "Spread your legs, damn it, I bet you're hiding a file! And the next time you wipe your ass, use the newspaper in the latrine, you hear me, you piece of shit? We're going back to your cell."

And the guard took him back. They went into the cell, and the guard told him, "Here are the clothes they brought you," and he threw a shirt and a pair of pants at him.

"Uncle Boris," Lucien thought, and a stream of life passed before his eyes. He managed to stand up and dragged himself to the window to get a breath of air. He saw the dim lights of Buenos Aires. Soon it would be light.

Everything about the rice field was so different from this world. I miss the land and working the fields, and I haven't forgotten the woods, or how hard it was to uproot the tenacious *caranday* trees, or that habit of yours of drinking a shot of pure alcohol at breakfast, a custom from your frozen homeland.

Father, I feel like the water in the rice field when it overflows the levee, but the rice retains water, the way I hold onto your words.

Case No. : 6695

The judgment of the alleged and concomitant crimes of the defendant, as well as those that may be charged later, will follow due process. This shall be recorded.

RESPONSABLE: CARLOS ONGARDA   AUTORIZACIÓN
N: 6695   R: 6

POLICE OF THE FEDERAL DISTRICT

Case No. 23 (Part One)
Buenos Aires, 8 January 1919
The Chief of Police of Investigations
Orders:
I. Summary Proceedings
II. Capture
I. CONFISCATION OF:
I.—One knife, 10 inches in length,
sharp point, black wooden handle, and
three yellow metal rivets, alleged weapon
used by the suspect Lucien Finz to wound
agent Camilo Uriburu, act committed the
morning of the 7th of this month, on
Sarmiento Street, at the corner of Callao,
at 11:00 A.M., according to the report to
the CHIEF OF INVESTIGATIONS.

II. The sum of $8.00, comprised of
one $5.00 bill, and the rest in $1.00
denominations, presumably stolen from
the basement of the former Café Richmond,
where the defendant was found.

III. A family photograph, presumably
that of the defendant's family.

IV. A sketch, presumably drawn by
the aforementioned, picturing two agents
carrying away a dangerous subject with a
pointed nose and thick eyeglasses.

V. A pair of black-and-white-striped
dress trousers, a wool jacket, an 18-carat
gold "Electra" watch, valued at $9.00.

VI. A briefcase with a nickel clasp
on one side, containing a "Luer" brand
syringe in a case, a stethoscope, a probe,
and a notebook marked "Anatomy." Report
ordered by THE CHIEF OF INVESTIGATIONS:
SUBMITTED ON THIS DATE.

II. CAPTURE:

Lucien Finz, Argentine, claims to be the son of Vasili Finz and Ana Yagupsky de Finz, both nationalized foreigners. White skin, light-brown hair, with a scar on his scalp, tall in stature, thin physique, wide forehead, straight nose, arched wide-set eyebrows, ordinary eyelids, blue eyes, thin lips, pronounced jawbone, medium-sized ears with large lobes, clean-shaven, reads and writes, claims to be a medical student and employee of the railway. Fingerprint V. 4343. The information recorded herein concerns the defendant who goes by the name Lucien Finz. Report ordered by THE CHIEF OF INVESTIGATIONS: SUBMITTED ON THIS DATE.

The report said I worked for *La Protesta* and the anarchists' cause, and that I was an activist without a trade, and a criminal with neither morals nor homeland.

The policeman shuffled some papers on his desk and said, "I'm going to set you free . . . trust me. With a little luck, all this will be over tonight."

Once again, he remembered what his father had told him about Czar Nicholas II, that he walked like an army of caterpillars. And now Lucien saw the officer the way his father saw Czar Nicholas II.

Father, why did you say you couldn't live without working the land? Everyone working from the crack of dawn . . . but I felt trapped in the rice field.

I see you again, Father, deep in thought, as you hold my little hand. The fog slips over your worn hands, and I look with the eyes of a child at your long fingers, and we enter the cemetery. You place a round stone on my mother's tomb, and I lay another one there, smaller and rounder than yours.

You speak to the tomb in a low voice, pronouncing the words with emotion, "An army of caterpillars devoured the rice crop," and you go on to say, "And if it doesn't rain, we'll lose the rice plants. And if it rains too much, the seeds will rot. . . ." Your hoarse voice still resounds here in my ears.

Why did you speak that way at my mother's grave, mixing Yiddish, Spanish, and Hebrew?

I see you again, Father, standing by the tombstone, dismayed, wearing your threadbare jacket, the same jacket you wore every winter, and your muddy rubber boots, regretting in a hush voice what God didn't help you save. "Oh God, do not reprehend me with your wrath, do not punish me with your fury!"

"Let's go back, Lucien, the pampero's blowing," you tell me.

And once again, I hear you pump water to wash your hands, and I know that I too must wash my hands after visiting the dead. There's a wall covered in blooming morning glories, and a flight of scissor-tailed flycatchers soars through the air in a "V" formation.

You say to me, "It's going to rain again, but this time the wind won't catch me standing still. I'm going to work all night long until I finish digging the levees to hold back the water."

I gazed at the newly sprouted rice, and from above it seemed brown to me, but when I stooped down, I could see the green shoots. By the holidays, the flowers would bend over, and you'd watch us as we laughed, but you never laughed, always on guard, with the stillness of a lizard under attack, as if Max, Noé, and I were nothing more than squanderers, ungrateful for life.

"That's enough now, you act like you have it all," you'd say.

Max and Noé teased you, but you, Father, stayed firm, as if your body were shielded, as if laughter would be a betrayal of your duty as a diligent rice farmer.

Anything that was not Villa Clara was not part of this world. Your whole world was this tiny village, your little parcel of land, the rural co-op whose advice you followed, and you felt that this was the way it should be for all the farmers.

Whenever the army of caterpillars returned to attack us, you'd sleep in your clothes, and awaken suddenly, and charge into the rice field in a rage, as if it were possible to wipe out that entire tangle of slippery green worms. You were tireless and stubborn in your old age, Father.

I remember when I was a boy, I'd wrap myself up in your wool jacket. It was just as cold as it surely was that morning you left the Black Sea. . . . But, for you, the vast steppe was a blurred map in your memory.

I'm grateful that you taught me to always be true to myself.

Father, you also spoke of David, who died of tuberculosis soon after he arrived in Colonia Clara. Your brother David had been a butcher, and you said that he followed the Jewish ritual for slaughtering to the letter, and that he had a sharp knife, and could butcher an animal quickly.

Once again I see a door with a frosted pane, and behind it the shadow of the officer, outlined against the wall. He tells another shadow that I have four broken vertebrae, and that the burns on my chest from the hot iron are third degree.

The shadow threatens me for a long time.

The officer enters the cell and looks at him, with his legs spread apart. "Finz, just remember, you didn't suffer any mistreatment."

Lucien sinks into his cot.

"That anarchist pig brainwashed you, Finz."

Again Lucien hears the cries of a prisoner howling in the next cell, and he covers his ears. His entire memory dissolves beneath a rainfall of books, crashing inside his head once more, like the day those plainclothes policemen entered the Jewish quarter and piled hundreds of books and set them on fire, and then dragged Lucien to that ungodly place where there was nothing but rats.

I endure the pain now the way I did when I dislocated my shoulder after falling off the horse, and I felt that brutal pain throughout my body. It was a long time before I could go back to pitching the hay that grew in the marsh. What an ugly ochre color that hay was, Father. And I'm still a wretched rice farmer clinging stubbornly to life. If only I could speak to you face to face. . . .

A guard brought him a plate of rice. Lucien said he was not hungry, and the guard asked him, "What's the matter, don't you like rice?"

"Shit . . . !" Lucien muttered, as he restrained himself to keep from insulting the guard.

Lucien threw the rice on the floor.

They let him go out to an enclosed courtyard. One of the guards told him he had seen the Jewish neighborhood burn, and that piles of books and belongings went up in flames in the street. His entire history, and that of his grandparents, came down on him like an avalanche of snow.

Later, a sergeant read to him the report that accused the anarchists of the assault on the 26th District Precinct, and he hoped his Uncle Boris was looking for him in all the police stations of Buenos Aires.

Lucien dreams that the officer is chasing him with a knife and screaming at him, "I only want one of your ears." Lucien runs the length of the waterfront, covering his ear with his hand. He sees himself amid hundreds of trunks piled along the wharf, and does not hesitate to open the lid of a trunk and hide in it. When the officer finds him, Lucien notices it is morning and the guards have changed shifts.

Lucien tells the guard he has to urinate and manages to stand up. He drags his feet as the guard accompanies him to the latrine in the next courtyard.

While he drinks from the faucet, he hears the moans of a prisoner, and thinks he recognizes the cries of his friend Luigi.

Now I'm a dreadful criminal who's not even given a chance to defend himself. I couldn't say any more because nothing I might tell you seems anything like what's happening to me. I believe I'm still in the rice field, it's a hot day, and I'm bending over the field with a shovel in my hand. A storm's brewing, and I must turn the dirt over with the shovel, and I pray the plants won't drown. I look at the rice, falling over with its plump grains, and my eyes see everything rotting away with so much rain, and sun, and silence.

Once again I see the white shape, with black eyes and a thin mustache, moving above the skylight. He squeezes my jugular with his hand.

Then he seems to hear his father telling him, "Lucien, cut the rice stalks low and store them here."

Silence. He can no longer hear what else Vasili Finz says.

I watch a flight of scissor-tailed flycatchers soar across the white sky, a fragile, sunny mirage, and I know all this is no longer for me. I take one last look at the rice field. The black earth, the sprouts of rice that captivate me with their splendor, and that familiar vague odor, like the foul smell of animals about to be slaughtered, and all this confirms there's nothing for me in Villa Clara.

The buzzer rings in the cell, and Lucien does not know if he is himself or someone else, and when he reacts, he sees behind the frosted pane the shadowy face of a man with a white lab coat telling him to open his mouth.

I open my mouth and swallow the castor oil the man in the white coat gives me. He shows me an illuminated box and asks me my name. I hesitate and don't respond. I recognize that voice. He says, "Your silence is older than misery. . . . Laws were written to be carried out, and as a Jew you should know what it means to disobey the law."

Neither the threats nor the torture to which that man subjected him will determine his fate, and Lucien tells him he is not going to obey a false law that he invented for his own use. Then the man takes him down a dark corridor that leads into a room smelling of ether. Now he is certain that the man in white who is speaking to him is the Civil Guard officer. He says, "Neither the Maximalists nor the anarchists want laws because the law is an obstacle to satisfying their desires to spread terror throughout the nation."

Lucien sees the man rub his thin gold ring with his thumb, and stick out his tongue, like an animal licking itself. He orders Lucien to undress. A scalpel shines in his hands, and he looks Lucien over from head to toe and asks him, "Were you circumcised?"

"Yes."

"Well, we're going to do it again."

And suddenly, he shoves a mask full of ether over his face. Lucien vaguely remembers that he saw something like a faint sun hidden behind thick clouds.

I can hear the sound of thunder splitting the night, like the burn that splits the soles of my feet. The guard asks if I smoke. I tell him my chest hurts when I breathe. He says the Civil Guard officer asked about me.

I don't see that man again, but he knows that wherever I am, I will think about him.

IV
NEITHER BEFORE NOR AFTER

Gathered here in the Naval Center, under the command
of Admiral Domeq García, and with the unconditional
support of Monsignor Andrea, we join together
under the name of Defenders of Order, with the mission of
forming armed civil brigades to confront the strikers.
—*THE PATRIOTIC LEAGUE, FEBRUARY 1920*

They allowed Uncle Boris to visit me. Sunday afternoon he came, and when he saw me, he held me for a long time, putting his arms around my neck. He brought me a razor and shaving cream, and convinced them to let me have Testut's *Anatomy* and Gley's *Physiology*. He also brought me a book by Montaigne, but I can't concentrate on the reading.

Uncle Boris said that the railway union lodged a complaint and is going to demand explanations from Yrigoyen for the atrocities committed against me in here.

Buenos Aires is filled with shadowy men whose fingerprints are not registered in any police office. Tomorrow the union lawyer's coming. Uncle Boris also said that the lawyer filed a protection order on my behalf as a political prisoner, and that the union will pay the defense lawyer. The railway workers, along with the other unions, called for another general strike in order to stop those who call themselves defenders of order, and who, in the name of patriotism, murder men, women, and children.

Uncle Boris says that the dissatisfaction with the government has never been greater than it has been this week. He says that what happened during these days is proof of how corrupt everything has become. He also said Yrigoyen promised freedom to all prisoners, and that he's going to investigate the men from the Civil Guard who are responsible for so many deaths.

Now, Buenos Aires is like a vague promise.

Laws: I don't believe in authorities who know nothing about what happened. When I get out, I'm going to find out what happened to me, so that no one will ever say again what I said to Luigi Melle the day I met him: "I don't get involved in politics."

There was a way out, but it took me a while to find it.

A guard asked me, "And now that you're free, what are you going to do, Russky?"

I took pleasure in glaring at him and not answering. It was almost dark. I walked along the wall and saw some boys smoking and laughing. I hurried and vanished from that place.

At that moment, Lucien remembers walking home with his father. In the sunlight, the air and the dust were blinding.

Lucien told Vasili he did not want to work in the rice field anymore. His father's eyes glistened like the blade of a knife, and he said nothing. Finally, he told Lucien that he hoped he would do well in Buenos Aires.

When he got to Plaza Italia, Lucien thought, "If I keep living on the fringes of what goes on in this city, I'll be lonelier in Buenos Aires than I was in Villa Clara. Rice matures in February, neither before nor after."

In prison, you see the other side of life. I suppose, Father, that I have been a selfish fool. I refused to listen to the voices of the workers who were outside these walls. I return to the world of the living, and I swear I'll be on their side and against the indifference of those dark characters I can't possibly avoid.

I want you to know, Father, that during the seven days my arrest lasted, I needed to speak to you, as if I were writing a long letter I never wrote you, with words I never spoke that kept spilling from my mouth until none were left.

Gusts blew hard from the river, and Lucien struggled to walk against that southeasterly wind. As he wandered down a deserted street, he heard the soft rumble of a train in the distance.

*"My father, Lucien Finz, worked as a country doctor near Villa Clara, where he spent his childhood. He intended to write his memoirs, but never did."**

---

* From a manuscript signed by Leonora Finz, recently found in the Lucienville Public Library in Basavilbaso, Entre Ríos, July 29, 2001.

COMPLOT

In the beginning of the Argentine tragedy, there is a drop
of blood and one of semen, product of the original rape.
—*Ezequiel Martínez Estrada*

*I would like to acknowledge the support of Beatriz Mauro,
also that of Sergio Aguirre, Gastón Sironi,
Márgara Averbach, Susana Cabuchi,
my translator, Rhonda Dahl Buchanan,
and my mentor, Andrés Rivera.*

I

May 24, 1932

A s she saddles her horse, Mora hears her grandmother telling her, "Go, my child, and don't tarry. I already spoke with your Aunt Luisa. Go get your clothes."

The girl ties a white ribbon in a knot around the end of her dark braid, mounts, and leaves. As she rides through the marsh, the water splashes under the animal's hoofs. Mora looks back and sees her grandmother getting smaller and smaller, until she finally disappears.

The Edelses' ranch is about nine miles from Colón. The girl breaks into a gallop and heads down the dirt road. It has been raining and the shoulders of the road are muddy and wet. Mora stays in the tracks where the dirt is not so slippery. She remembers that her father, Jordán, is in Pago Largo, and she does not know why that makes her happy. She quickens her pace and decides to take a short cut, riding near Pueblo Liebig, before turning toward the river. As she crosses the Maldonado, the stream's high water comes rushing toward them, and the horse rears. She pulls on the reins, and the animal charges through the water and swims. Mora holds onto the horse's mane until they reach the other shore, then grabs the reins and gallops again across the fields.

Mora hears the shrill whistle of an approaching train. The ground trembles and the sky turns black with smoke. She reaches the railroad crossing and finds the gates lowered. She pulls on the reins, and the horse digs into the ground and waits. The train advances slowly, then stops at the crossing, spitting out embers and ash as it moves on.

Mora is hungry. Her hair gets in her eyes, and she blows it away. When the gates rise, she crosses the tracks and ventures across the flat, even plain. She spurs her horse on, thinking she will make it to La Lucera in just a few more miles. The rancid smell of the Yussim dairy fills the air, and a warm, muggy breeze starts to blow.

When she gets to the ranch, Mora opens the gate and rides through the orange grove, then past the eucalyptus trees. She comes to a halt in front of Eli's house, and finds it strange the dogs are not there, nor the rancher's Chevy *Voituré*. She gets off her horse, walks to the door, and knocks. No one answers, and Mora hears the grunting of the hogs in the pigsty and the churning of the water mill. No one is home, and the girl decides to wait for Eli.

She walks around to the back of the house. The sheets on the clothesline sway in the breeze, and the chickens are asleep in the shade. Mora sits down on a fallen tree trunk and watches some ants file into an anthill. She takes a piece of bread out of her pocket and devours it. Then she goes over to the pond and scoops some water into her collapsible cup. The goldfish stir in the rippling water, and something inside Mora also stirs and swims. She quenches her thirst, then closes the cup, covers it, and puts it in the pocket of her long wool shirt. Suddenly, she hears a shot ring out from the barn. It startles her and the horse, and when she looks up she sees a man running from the barn and recognizes him: it is her father. She stares at him until Jordán disappears behind the cornfield, and then she wonders why he told her that the Englishman had sent him to drive the herd to Pago Largo. Mora enters the barn and sees an empty basin on a table. The girl takes a few uneasy steps on the hard dirt floor and the door creaks. Her eyes travel from the shovels to the silo, while horseflies dart around her. Mora sees the old man sitting on the seat of the reaper with his back toward her. "He has on that flannel shirt he always wears," she thinks. She moves nearer: the old man's neck is shiny, his face oily, his mouth open. The girl muffles a cry when she sees the man up close and realizes that he is the *patrón*, Eli's father, dead with a bullet wound to the chest.

Tobe, the hunting dog, whimpers at his master's side. She stands there looking at that man. There is no longer any fury in his eyes or his hands.

After catching her breath, she runs, and mounts her horse, and as she flees, she remembers her father was in the Edelses' house when she served tea to the Englishman and Elsa Kessler. She hears the sound of an approaching horse. It is the police inspector from Colón, who asks her where she is coming from. It is a polite question, but Mora, her eyes lowered, licks her lips and says she has been picking fennel. He tells her in a commanding voice to go home.

The girl's house sits in the heart of La Lucera. When she gets there, she goes to her room, lies on her bed, and thinks about that old man who is dead now. And she remembers when she wanted to tell Aunt Luisa what was happening, but could not, and told her instead that she did not like the patrón, that he was a son of a bitch because he beat Eli, and Aunt Luisa told her to be quiet.

Her father, sitting in the cane chair next to the iron stove, asks her, "What does my girl want to eat?"

"I'm not hungry."

She gets out of bed, walks away slowly, and leaves. Jordán asks her where she is going, and she says she wants to fetch water from the well.

Mora sees the water trickling down the ditch, picks some calla lilies, then steps through the barbed-wire fence and heads into the open field. On her way back to the farm, she hears the roar of Eli's father's Chevy Voituré coming toward her with the top down. The girl sees Elsa Kessler at the wheel, beautiful but cold. An amber-colored scarf flutters at her neck. Eli waves at her and smiles.

II

His name was Bruno Edels and he lived with his family in Prague. When his parents were murdered in a pogrom, his sisters Ana and Lena escaped to France, and he found refuge with a family of farmers in the Russian village of Tsarkoye Selo, where he fell in love with Olga Gumiliov. When she was shot for treason against the almighty Czar of Russia, he had to flee, and crossed the Black Sea to the port of Athens. He worked there as a stevedore, and later as a boatswain on a Turkish ship. He was twenty-five years old.

December 1903

Bruno Edels managed to obtain passage on a cargo ship going to America. While in the port of Buenos Aires, a stranger told him that if he was looking for work he could find it in Entre Ríos. After that, Edels headed for the Retiro Station.

When he stepped off the train, he felt like a child who awakens and does not understand what is happening. He walked along the platform and crossed the street. His eyes scanned the houses dotting the plain, and for a moment, he forgot how exhausted he was.

Before long, Bruno Edels had settled in Colón. There he began working the land without rest, as a farmhand, fence builder, and butcher. He learned to read and write Spanish on his own, and it was strange to hear how he dragged out the letter *rr*, and pronounced his words forcefully, elongating the syllables.

One afternoon while he was sitting around after work with the other farmhands, one of them asked him what Prague was like. He pretended he had not heard him, and said he was saving up to bring his sisters over. That was all he said.

Those first years, through personal sacrifices, he saved enough money to rent a parcel of land. He grew wheat and produced an abundant harvest of grain. With the money from the sale of wheat he bought a flour mill, and with the profits he earned from the mill he bought cows and horses. He became a powerful landowner, master of La Lucera and El Chajá, ranches near the Uruguay River.

January 1916

Edels received a letter from Olga Gumiliov's brother telling him that Ana and Lena had been murdered in a mysterious incident. At that moment he was struck by the futility of his long wait and the tremendous exhaustion he had borne since the night he was separated from his sisters.

In Colón, rumors began to circulate that the rich Jew, who was nearly forty and had never married, had become a womanizer who had a taste for young girls and made shameless advances toward them. He also tried to seduce the wife of a sergeant from Basavilbaso, and was nearly stabbed to death, but managed to appease the husband by slipping a bill in his pocket.

December 1919

He saw her for the first time at the wheat festival. She walked past him under the filtered glow of the red paper lanterns. Her blond hair fell over her wide forehead, lending her an air of an unattainable woman. He asked who that girl was, and they told him she was the daughter of Herr Kessler, the baker from Urdinarrain. She was about fifteen years younger than he, and her body, fair skin, and blue eyes reminded him of Olga Gumiliov. A storm brewed within him as he approached her, smiling, and offered her a glass of wine. Elsa Kessler looked him straight in the eye and told him rather flippantly that the wine was lousy. He spoke to her about La Lucera and El Chajá, the ranches he owned. She mentioned in passing that her parents had not always been poor. When she said she had to leave, he held her back and looked at her, with his mouth half-open, like a powerful animal confronting a female in heat.

Before long, he asked her to marry him, and with an unexpected softness in her voice, she accepted his proposal. Her parents did not hesitate to give him their daughter's hand, and they married soon thereafter.

The wedding brought together ranchers, farmers, and shopkeepers from the villages near La Lucera. Jordán, Edels's foreman and right-hand man, and his wife, the ranch's cook, organized the party. They grilled a whole steer, and there was music and horse racing, with the festivities lasting until dawn. That morning, Jordán's wife gave birth to a girl they named Mora.

Nine months later, Eli was born, the only son the Edelses had.

When the boy turned eight, his father rented El Chajá to Mister Broker, an Englishman who had once lived in the United States, in the Deep South. He was the legal advisor for the Entre Ríos Central Railways, and was rumored to have ties to influential bankers. As a generous gesture, Mister Broker offered to introduce Edels to those people.

Bruno Edels received a formal letter notifying him that a tract of El Chajá was to be expropriated, and a strip of La Lucera as well, so that a new stretch of railway could be laid to connect part of Mesopotamia with the port of Buenos Aires.

Bruno Edels had no intention of parting with that land. Furious, he went to see Mister Broker with the letter in hand, and said to him, "Do something, use your influence!"

"In exchange for what?"

"You tell me, Mister Broker."

"You sell El Chajá to me."

"No. El Chajá is not for sale."

The Englishman filled his pipe and said, "If my proposal doesn't suit you, then handle your own matters with the State."

"Don't play both hands at once, Mister Broker."

"I'm not playing, just fulfilling my duties."

Sitting at the other side of the desk, anxious, his face weary, Bruno Edels did not respond.

Mister Broker served him a glass of whiskey and then said, "See here, Edels, accept the deal. You know the State's more powerful than you. They'll pay you in sterling pounds. Do you have any idea how much that land will appraise for with that stretch of tracks cutting through it?"

Edels thought about it.

"Why don't we talk this over calmly another day, and we'll see what can be gained from all of this?" the Englishman said. Then he paused and added, "I invite you to go duck hunting and we can talk about it then."

"Agreed, but instead of hunting ducks, I'd rather fish for *dorado*."

"I hear there are some ferocious rivals in that river that can be tempted with the right bait."

"In fishing, there's always one who deceives, and one who is deceived."

"But there has to be a lure between them, a live bait," replied the Englishman.

"It's not easy to catch a dorado, Mister Broker," Edels went on to say. "It has a tough mouth, and you have to hook it twice."

The Englishman remarked, "In the British Museum we have lures made of chicken feathers and . . ."

Edels interrupted him, "I don't want to hear that! Fishing's not a game. . . ."

"Very well, enough said."

Edels suggested they leave at dawn, and the Englishman agreed.

Mister Broker heard the sound of boots as Edels walked to the door, and the Englishman let him show himself out.

A few days later, the Argentine Land and Investment Company Limited sent Sir Alfred Armington as a representative member of the Board of Directors of the Railways to interview Edels, as stipulated by the laws of England, and in a matter of weeks, a contract was signed to expropriate the land.

N⁰ 205202

UN PESO
1 PESO
Año 1930

PUBLIC DEED NUMBER ONE HUNDRED TWENTY THREE.—In the city of Colón, Department of Colón, Province of Entre Ríos, Argentine Republic, the seventh of November of nineteen hundred and thirty.—Hereby summoned before me, an authorized Notary Public, and the undersigned witnesses are: the first party, Mister ALFRED ARMINGTON, who signs his name "Sir Alfred Armington," current resident of the city of Buenos Aires, of this Republic; and the second party, Mr. BRUNO EDELS, who signs his name "B. L. Edels," resident of this Department, both married once, of legal age, and persons of my acquaintance. I do solemnly swear that Mister Edels agrees to this contract of his own free will, as does Mister Armington, as representative of the company founded in England under the name of the "ARGENTINE LAND AND INVESTMENT COMPANY LIMITED."—The bylaws of said company and its official acknowledgment as a legal entity, are hereby transcribed in the Public Business Registry of the City of Concepción, Uruguay, on page one hundred forty-five, volume eleven of the Records of the year nineteen hundred and twenty-three; verifying the legal rights of Mister Armington to act in this capacity, with the Power of Attorney vested in him by Sir Cecil Constantine Easton, Director of the aforementioned Company, and the authorization granted him in writing by the aforementioned Director in the city of Buenos Aires, of this Republic, on the twenty-fourth of January of nineteen hundred and twenty-nine, before the Notary Public, Mister Jacinto J. Dórtegui, and appearing on page one hundred forty-two of Registry number three, under his jurisdiction, whose authority as a witness may be found transcribed in its entirety on deed number one hundred twenty-four, presented to me and now appearing in my Registry, with the date of the seventh of June of nineteen hundred and twenty-nine, and on page three hundred forty-three of the Record corresponding to the same year. I do solemnly swear that the deed in question is found to be in force in all respects, according to the certificate attached to the deed, which is recorded on page three hundred eighty-nine of this Registry and current Record, wherein this action is transcribed with all pertinent information, as follows: "Concerning the authorization granted in the City of London, in the Kingdom of England."— In the City of London, on the second of August of nineteen hundred and twenty-eight, before me, its Notary Public, Mister Henry Alfred Bridge, and the witnesses whose signatures appear below, are hereby summoned Mister Charles Byshire and Mister Stuart Colquhoum Sephard, two of the directors of the Company, established in this City, and legally founded and registered, according to the current laws of England, under the name of "Argentine Land and Investment Company Limited."— Furthermore, given that they act of their own free will, are rightly authorized, competent to execute this act, of legal age, residents of this city, and persons of my acquaintance, I verify that they act on their own behalf and on behalf of the other directors of the Company, under the powers granted them in articles 1 and 3, clause (9) of the Minutes of the Association, and Articles 62, clause (1), 63 and 64, clause (1) of the bylaws of the aforementioned company and by the respective agreements prescribed by the Board of Directors in its meetings, held on the seventh day of June of the present year. Included in the records is a Spanish translation of all articles and agreements, and the results of the election and last reelection of the aforementioned directors, as duly noted in the record book of said company,

which I have seen, and which states the following: "Minutes of the Association: 1) The legal name of the Company is 'Argentine Land and Investment Company Limited.'— . . . The objectives for which the Company is established are: (9) To administer, exploit, develop, profit, operate, sell, rent, mortgage, tax, transfer, or in other ways negotiate with any or all of the assets of the Company, and to administer, exploit, profit, operate, sell, rent, mortgage, tax, transfer, or dispose of in any way deemed necessary any other assets: real estate or possessions, business or firm, as well as agents of any company, individual or individuals."—Social Bylaws.— Article 62 (1)—The Board of Directors may grant at their discretion any Director, Supervisor or Supervisors, or any local advisory board, or any agent or representative of the Company the power and authority the Board esteems necessary for the effective management of the business matters of the Company, or of any other special matters, and may confer such power in writing, with or without the power of substitution, in favour of any person, property, or entity, or personnel, in order to sell, concede, and transfer all or part of the real estate property, urban or rural, of the Company located in any part of the Republic, for the cost or costs, either paid in full or by installments, and in accordance with all agreements, terms, and conditions established for the transaction. . . .

III

March 1930

Dawn breaks, announcing the first signs of autumn. The water laps against the dock, where Edels's boat is tied. The Englishman arrives at the dock, impeccably dressed, wearing a silk ascot around his neck, white riding pants, and boots. Edels also heads for the dock, his pale, tired face shaded by the wide brim of his hat.

He meets the Englishman and asks him how long he has been waiting. Mister Broker tells him that he has just arrived, and they walk to the boat together. Tobe, Edels's hunting dog, barks furiously at the Englishman. Edels shouts at him, "Tobe, lie down, now!" The dog howls, but obeys.

"What can I say, he just doesn't like you," Edels says.

Mister Broker gives him a strange look and asks, "What's your dog doing here?"

"He goes everywhere with me."

They board the boat and Edels puts a reel of fishing line next to the bait can. Then he grasps the throttle and they pull away from the dock. Tobe stays behind and watches as the boat heads toward the deeper water, cresting in the wind.

"How did you sleep, Mister Broker?"

"Very well."

"Do you want *mate*?"

"No."

The sun glistens like copper on the river. Reddish leaves float in the water. The Englishman sees some dirty barefoot children playing on the shore.

The boat heads into a patch of water darkened by a school of *surubí* breaking the surface. Edels veers south, and the Englishman watches an island of thick vegetation float past them. The wind picks up, and the vessel rocks.

"The water's very choppy," says the Englishman. "Will you give me a light?"

"I'm not smoking," says Edels. "It's time to fish."

The Englishman leans against the bow. His reddish hair shines in the morning light as he prepares his rod for casting. That river reminds him of another vast, forsaken river near the place he lived as a boy, a river he yearns for. After running a while, they reach a spot with a good current, and Edels cuts the boat's motor. The sky is clear, and the sound of moving water breaks the silence. A lapwing soars through the air, and suddenly the Englishman's vision becomes cloudy. He feels dizzy and lowers his head until the nausea passes.

"Do you feel all right, Mister Broker?"

"Yes."

"Have some cognac," Edels suggests.

The Englishman takes a sip and looks at him as if Edels were his father, and he a little boy who does what he is told to do.

"Get ready for the strike, my friend," Edels warns him, and begins to cut shad into pieces for bait. "Tell me something about yourself, Mister Broker."

"What can I tell you? . . . I'd rather talk business."

"Go ahead."

The Englishman starts to talk about the money they could make shipping beef to England.

"Lots of money, more than you can imagine, Edels. We should build a meatpacking plant."

"They already have one in Pueblo Liebig."

"And what does that matter?"

"And one in Fray Bentos."

"We'll earn more than the two of them together!"

Bruno Edels opens his eyes and asks, "And how much money would we need to invest?"

"You provide the land, and I'll take care of the rest," Mister Broker answers, and goes on to say that since order has been restored to the country, he has the contacts they will need in the government and the customs office.

"Explain this business to me in more detail," Edels says.

"We slaughter the cattle, preserve the meat, and ship the frozen quarters to England."

"It's that simple?"

"I know exactly what I'm talking about."

"And you, Mister Broker, what do you want out of this? What, while I sit back and do nothing?"

"I already told you what you have to do."

"I don't want to take any risks."

"But there are no risks!"

"Not for you, Mister Broker, with the Bank of London and South America backing you."

The Englishman explains, "The backing I have insures the business."

"Will the bank sign a policy that protects me?"

"That won't be necessary. You have my word."

"I need a guarantee in writing . . . without it, you can count me out."

"Just imagine, Edels, we can have a monopoly on the exportation of veal."

Edels thinks about it, but says nothing. Mister Broker adds, "Let's do this: if you're not interested in this business, forget about my proposal. You sell me a tract of El Chajá, and we'll still be friends."

"I already told you that El Chajá is not for sale."

He offers him more than El Chajá is worth, but Edels repeats that it is not for sale.

"I'll pay you double."

Edels does not respond.

The Englishman nails him with a glassy stare. "Tell me how much you want."

Edels takes off his hat, scratches his neck, hesitates, and finally says, "All right, if we go ahead with this meat business, we'll do it, but under certain conditions."

"Conditions? Listen, splitting the profits in half with you is more than generous on my part. Besides, who do you think will get the contacts to ship everything to England, and the sterling pounds we need to set up the plant?"

"I don't want to hear about sterling pounds, I want it in pesos," Edels insists.

"I'm telling you, the profits are going to be huge," says the Englishman.

"But won't the taxes eat up half the profits?"

"No, because we're only going to declare 20 percent of what we ship."

Mister Broker smiles, pauses for a moment, and says, "Do you have any idea how much money we're talking about?"

Edels contemplates that, his face anxious.

"No one's persecuting you here, Edels. We're in Argentina," the Englishman reminds him.

Edels does not know what to do, and finally says, "Let me think about it, Mister Broker."

"We have plenty of time."

While the Englishman prepares his line, he thinks about the railroad link that will connect the northern and eastern provinces of the country with the port of Buenos Aires. He has seen the blueprints for the train stations, the electrical plant, and the model for the railroad town. Everything is going to pass between La

Lucera and El Chajá, from Colón to the port of Buenos Aires. Edels knows nothing about this, nor does he know about the network of young flesh the Englishman traffics. He heads an organization that recruits young girls from the north and sends them to the high-class brothels in Buenos Aires.

The purr of a motorboat heading into deep water disturbs the silence. Edels baits the hook and says, "The reel has to be very tight, Mister Broker, and you need to pull hard when it strikes. Remember the dorado has a very tough mouth."

The Englishman prepares his rod to cast, and when he lets out the line, he remembers: "Father and the Mississippi. . . . The iron bridge over the river . . . the farm . . . mist, clouds . . . pine trees. The house on the shore of the river. And Mama is a shadow wandering along the porch. Voices in the dining room. Someone's singing 'Old Black Joe.' Later, when no one's there, not even old black Kay, Papa says to me, to the little boy I used to be, there, on the shores of the Mississippi, that he'll take me to my room. The smell of tobacco in the air. Suddenly, Papa's stroking me and taking off my clothes."

Then the image fades into darkness.

"What are you thinking about, Mister Broker?"

Startled, the Englishman says, "Nothing, nothing at all. . . . Tell me, Edels, the land behind the riverbank, it's yours, isn't it?"

Edels smiles.

"It's immense," says the Englishman.

"No, but I wish my land went all the way to Pago Largo, where Urquiza skinned Berón de Astrada. Have you ever heard that story, Broker?"

The Englishman does not reply.

Edels tells him that Urquiza made whips for his soldiers with the skin of that leader.

"Oh God!" Mister Broker mutters.

Edels offers him a cigar and says, "Get ready to do battle with the greatest fish in this river."

And he casts the line again. The Englishman does the same.

"When it circles round, keep the line tight, or else when the fish jumps, it will come unhooked," Edels advises him.

They wait a long time without speaking. Edels offers him *mate*, and the Englishman says he does not care for it.

"There's tea, Mister Broker." The Englishman accepts and serves himself a cup.

"Damn it, the wind's picking up," says Edels.

"So what? Remember that a rough river . . ."

"Yes, but the wind can make us drift."

Edels realizes that something has taken his bait, and he shouts, "I have it!" He reels in the line and sees it is a surubí.

"It's too small," he says, and throws it back into the river.

After a while, Edels hooks a dorado.

"It's enormous, and I really hooked him!" Edels shouts.

The dorado struggles for a few minutes, jumping in and out of the water. Once in the boat, it glistens, quivers, and finally stops moving.

"Now it's your turn to catch a big one," Edels tells him.

After a couple more hours of waiting, the men's faces are calm. To pass the time, they talk about women, and the Englishman confesses that he loses sleep over Madame Ricard.

"So you like her?"

The Englishman says he does. He thinks about that woman, her knack for documenting the girls who she declares are going to work as maids for the best families of Buenos Aires. Madame Ricard gets the contracts, and knows what to do if someone in the family finds out where one of the young girls ends up.

The conversation is interrupted when the Englishman's line becomes taut. He pulls with all his might, and a powerful dorado breaks out of the water, hooked on his lure. The Englishman cannot contain himself and shouts, "I feel the . . . I feel . . . !"

"What are you saying?"

"Nothing . . . nothing."

The fish is bigger than the one Edels caught, and the

Englishman cannot take his eyes off it, and exclaims, "It's the finest catch I've ever seen in my life!"

Edels barely smiles.

"This deserves a toast," says Mister Broker.

"Let's drink to it," says Edels.

IV

My father was fourteen years old when Bruno Edels had him plant those rows of eucalyptus trees from the banks of the river all the way to where El Chajá ends at the edge of the forest. He said it was hard work chopping down the underbrush with a machete, and planting tree after tree, just so others could come along and fell what he had planted. Of course, he could have cut one of them down with a single blow.

My father always did what the patrón expected of him. He stayed there, at La Lucera, for more than twenty years, and was promoted to foreman around the time hardwood from the *peteribí* trees started to make money for the patrón. He told me about the men who would spend the entire day in the woods cutting down trees, and those who gathered the trunks of those freshly cut trees late into the night. Then he said that other workers would bind the logs with vines, or ropes made from esparto grass, and launch the rafts into the Uruguay to be carried away by the current. When the rafters left, all that remained on that shore, smooth and unbroken like the river, was the bark of the trees and a long silence.

Later, some of those men would return, bringing back things stolen from the Paraguay border. They'd hide them in the woods and then send them down the Uruguay to the Río de la Plata. My father warned me not to go into the woods alone, saying that it was dangerous for a little girl.

One night, Eli and I saw those men. We were on the riverbank when we heard strange grunts coming from the muddy shore. Eli looked at me, frightened, and I looked at him; something was moving down there. We thought it could be mountain lions sniffing around in the sand, so we stayed still, waiting for something to happen, our eyes staring into the darkness. There was a strong musky scent in the air. I wanted to tell Eli that we should leave, but I didn't say anything. We felt weak in the knees, but the tall, dense thicket protected us.

About ten strong men carrying boxes and kerosene lanterns walked by, panting, with quick, clumsy steps. We heard the noise the boxes made as they banged into each other. Then those strangers went deep into the woods.

The next day I went back there, and the ground was all trampled, as if a herd of wild boars had dug it up with their powerful snouts. And I remembered what my father had warned me, "If you come across one of those men, don't speak to him." My father didn't tell me that he was afraid they'd rape me, and there are things that a girl doesn't ask her father. We didn't speak about my mother, either, after she abandoned us. I was eight then, and I remember.

One morning, someone said she'd run off with one of those rafters who smuggled things down the Uruguay. And at the ranch they said she'd run off with a man my father knew, a farmhand from Domínguez my father had taught to make fences, someone I'd seen once from a distance. I believe my father went after her, but I'm not sure about that. He said she'd never come back, and that he'd gone to Colón to get Aunt Luisa to take care of me and do the cooking. I remember my father got rid of her clothes. I was afraid she was dead. Many times I wondered where my mother was, if she was still living. Maybe my father knew more about her than what he told me. I waited for him to speak about it, but he never did. Whatever happened, the earth swallowed my mother.

V

I remember the day I began to hate Bruno Edels. Once again, I hear his muddy boots pounding the tile floor, and him screaming, "Where in the hell is your mother?"

And Eli remained silent, and Bruno Edels, his face pale with fury, grabbed him by the ear and demanded again that he tell him where she was. Edels pushed Eli to his knees and started beating him with his whip, and yelling at him, nearly breathless, "You son of a bitch!" And I heard the crack of the whip on Eli's body.

It didn't matter to that old man that I was there. Nothing mattered to that old man.

From that moment on, I couldn't get it out of my head. After Edels left, slamming the door behind him, I went with Eli to the river. He sat down on the sand, his legs bent, his chin on his knees, motionless. I sat down beside him, and wanted to say something to him, but couldn't think of anything.

"I'm going to kill him," he told me.

Deep inside I believed that was what he had to do to his father, but I told him he shouldn't talk that way, that those were things better said . . .

"I'm on your side," I told him.

I didn't know what else to say.

"Who do you like, Mora?"

"I'm not going to tell you now."

I'm not sure how much time passed, how long we were there, silent, by the river. I only know that I remembered something I'd heard, that the Englishman was Elsa Kessler's lover.

It was raining gently. My father hadn't come home yet. I stood there looking out the window for a long time at that dreary afternoon, not knowing what to do. I waited for a while.

It stopped raining, and a swarm of butterflies flew out of the trees. The siren of the meatpacking plant startled me. I heard Tobe barking, and then the sound of a motor, and I saw Elsa Kessler get out of the Englishman's jeep. She was wearing a green blouse, and her hair was a lighter blond than usual. I waved at her, and she waved back and went into her house.

I felt like swimming, so I walked past the eucalyptus trees to the riverbank. That afternoon the Uruguay was tinged a bright red color. I went down the path to the shore. Dark eddies swirled in the river. I was tempted to dive in and swim, but then pools of blood and scraps of meat came floating by. I stepped back and saw the Englishman staring at me. He lit a cigar, exhaled a mouthful of smoke, and asked me what I was doing there. I told him I wanted to go swimming, but the water was dirty and very rough. He told me that, as a boy, he'd lived for many years by a river called the Mississippi, a river as endless and turbulent as the Uruguay.

His cigar trembled between his long, manicured fingers. His eyes glistened and his mouth was slightly twisted. I decided to go home. On the way, I thought about that meat floating by, and remembered the inauguration of the meatpacking plant. I didn't know what it was like inside. My father said it was equipped with machinery Mister Broker had brought from Great Britain.

The party was held at La Lucera, in the barn near the new railroad tracks. Eli wasn't there. I had to help Aunt Luisa and didn't leave the kitchen all afternoon.

The Englishman and Edels spent the entire day giving orders. The staff at the ranch waited on the guests, who arrived from Buenos Aires and other places: distinguished gentlemen, officers in their dress uniforms, and with them, their wives, who got out of the cars wearing linen blouses, long necklaces, bracelets, and expensive shoes. Some wore veiled hats, and left lipstick marks on their glasses. I'd never seen so many people in one place, as I did that night. Aunt Luisa and I observed those curious people who spoke and laughed and seemed happy.

The meatpacking plant was illuminated. The siren sounded for a long time. When the priest cut the ribbon, everyone applauded, and the guests sat down. There was laughter and the scent of perfume in the air. Bruno Edels thanked everyone for coming, and the Englishman gave a speech. There was more applause. They drank and ate: platters of salads, grilled intestines, strips of meat. They emptied their wine glasses. The women laughed, and the men unbuttoned their shirt collars.

The orchestra began to play waltzes while Mister Broker and Bruno Edels mingled among the guests. Edels, with his halting gait, waddled like a duck. It was the only time I ever saw him in a suit.

Elsa Kessler was beautiful. Everyone complimented her, and she seemed pleased as she sashayed about in her tight, clinging skirt. At one point, I saw her talking to a gentleman who, they said, had just arrived from London. I saw when Edels introduced her to him.

"Sir Alfred Armington, at your service, my lady," said that well-mannered man with a faint smile. She offered her hand.

"Call me Elsa," she said as she raised a glass of white wine to her lips.

That gentleman fixed his gaze on her cleavage. The two of them stood there talking together for a long time. Then I heard Elsa Kessler introduce him to her guests as "My friend, Alfred, a great polo player." That came to an end when a woman walked over and said, "Will you come here, Alfred?"

"I'm coming," he said, a bit uneasy.

Elsa Kessler threw her head back and went over to where Mister Broker was speaking with another guest. They were discussing a book.

"What are you talking about?" Elsa Kessler asked.

"About Milton, my lady," said the guest.

She did not respond.

I was putting some plates on the table when Mister Broker called me, "Mora, come here."

I went over, apprehensive of those men in their silk vests, smoking cigars and drinking whiskey. The Englishman said, "Bring more ice."

They looked me over from head to toe. I felt them undress me with their eyes, and was embarrassed.

"Girl, go to the jeep, and bring me the blue notebook you find there," said the Englishman.

I went to the jeep, and when I had the notebook in my hands, I read:

Shipment on the 1st of April of 1931
La Lucera—Liverpool
Steamship Lord Carnavon
Departure: 9:00

Frozen quarters: corned beef and canned goods.
Dried beef blood, ground meat for fertilizer, cracklings, lard, suet, brains, liver extract, hides, bristles, horns, hoofs, ear hairs, bones, glands, pancreas, ovaries, testicles, concentrated bile, kidneys, sweetbreads, livers. Stripped ribs and other boiled bones, gall bladders, and dried and salted tracheas in oak barrels. Beef bouillon. Organ meats.
Remaining for consumption in this country: intestines and tongues.

Shipment on the 1st of April of 1931
La Lucera—Río de Janeiro—Recife
Chalana El Palmar
Departure: 17:00
Beef jerky.

I closed the notebook and went back to the party. I saw that the Englishman was still talking to those men in the silk vests, and I heard them toast the president and the president's wife. When I went over to give him the notebook, I heard Elsa Kessler calling me, "Mora, bring another pitcher of *clericó*," and I obeyed.

The sun was coming up when the last guests left.

VI

My father and I rode our horses slowly, where the mud was packed down, without taking our eyes off the tracks. The road to Colón ran along the river. When we crossed the bridge, I saw Bruno Edels's boat tied to the dock, and I thought about that old man, and cursed him.

My father told me he was going to accompany the Englishman to get the yacht he'd bought in Buenos Aires, and he also said, "How long am I going to keep working for the Edelses, and what am I going to get out of all this?" He remembered the Englishman had proposed that he work for him, and that he'd pay him more money: it was his opportunity.

Ever since my mother left him for someone else, I believed we'd never move from La Lucera, but that wasn't what happened. My father said, "I want a better life for you now, my child."

I smiled at him and wondered how my father was going to give me a better life. It was obvious he knew what he was saying when he told me that.

We rode for a while, in silence, along the cemetery wall. My father asked me, "What's my girl thinking about?"

"Nothing. . . ."

"Oh, my little girl has a secret."

I smiled.

"What do you want to be when you grow up?"

"A teacher, father."

We left the bridge behind, and in the distance we saw the lights of the city shimmering by the river. When we reached Colón, we headed for the park. The entrance was illuminated with little red and yellow spotlights that turned on and off.

"Look at all the lights, Mora," my father said, and he stayed there blinking his eyes under the bright glow of the lamps, with his hat in his hand.

I looked around in amazement and saw some girls flying through the air in whirling seats, and I stood there, listening to their screams and laughter blended with the hoarse voice of a man singing, "*Titina, oh, Titina . . .*" Then we walked over to a booth, where a woman gave us some colored rings in exchange for a ticket. I tried to throw them over the bottlenecks, but missed. We continued walking, without speaking, through the wandering crowd.

"Ten cents for a spin around the world!" shouted a boy standing on a platform.

My father bought me a ticket, and I got on. I couldn't believe how the Ferris wheel moved. We all leaned back, with our faces to the wind, until the wheel came to a stop.

Once on the ground again, I waited. My father had told me that when I got off, I should stay there, and he'd come back and get me. I looked at the man who was operating the wheel with a lever and talking to a boy with an oily face. When the man saw me, he winked at the boy and asked me, "Do you want to ride, baby? If you suck me, I'll let you on."

Both of them laughed, and I ran away, trembling, to find my father. When I saw him, I felt the blood rush back to my body.

"You're all flushed, what's wrong with you?"

"Nothing."

"What does my little girl want to do now?"

"Go home." And I held his hand.

"Let's get some lemonade first."

We emptied the glasses of lemonade, got our horses, and went down the road that stretched on and on.

VII

It had been raining, but later the sun bathed the countryside. It was autumn and still warm. Bruno Edels told my father the place he'd chosen to hunt ducks was a few miles from El Chajá.

Herb, Mister Broker's Labrador, ran ahead and jumped into the truck before us. Then the Englishman, the patrón, my father, and Eli and I climbed in. My father wasn't happy that I was going with them, but he let me come along because they allowed Eli to go also.

The truck started up. Tobe and the other dogs from the ranch followed us for a while, until we lost sight of them. There was mud everywhere and the road was slick. We saw a train cross the iron bridge on its way to Ibicuy, and we turned onto a narrow road. We drove for a long time, and when we came to a marsh where the rushes were tall, the patrón stopped the truck and said it was a good spot to hunt ducks.

When we got out, Herb began to sniff the ground, and Mister Broker followed him. I asked Eli, "Why does Mister Broker have a rifle instead of a shotgun?"

"How should I know?" he answered.

Bruno Edels and Mister Broker discussed the best shells to use when the wind was blowing softly, as it was then. Eli and I put on rubber boots and hung canteens around our necks. We walked through a flooded and deserted hay field. I looked around, but couldn't see anything that would make anyone think this was a good place to hunt ducks. At the far end of the field, I saw a row of bare trees that looked like crippled men climbing the ravine. We jumped over the barbed-wire fence and trudged through the mud.

While the three men loaded shells into the chambers of their guns, Eli and I stuck poles into the ground and placed decoys on top. Then we hid among the tallest rushes and waited patiently for a long time. Finally, a flight of ducks appeared and circled the poles where we had placed the decoys. I remember that I held my breath when I saw the ducks, with their wings spread and their necks extended, as they approached the decoys. The men took aim and shot, and a few ducks fell into the middle of the lagoon. The Englishman released Herb, shouting at him to fetch, and the dog ran and retrieved the catch, one bird after another.

The Englishman looked at that shapeless, bloody thing whose feathers moved in the wind, and asked the patrón, "So how do you prepare these birds?"

"After cleaning them, I marinate them in honey and white wine, and then roast them."

"Always over a low flame, Mister Broker," my father added.

The smell of wet feathers filled the air. They kept hunting until the sun started to go down. We decided to return, but couldn't because we were stuck in the mud. We pushed the truck and its wheels spun and dug themselves even deeper into the mud. My father said he'd go for help, and left.

A herd of Axis deer was visible in the distance, and the sky was aglow under a veil of red and violet clouds. A phosphorescent light shimmered over the lagoon.

"There could be a buried treasure there," Edels murmured.

"What?" the Englishman asked.

"They say that where you see an eerie light, you'll find a buried boot filled with silver."

The Englishman laughed.

"You don't believe me, Broker?"

"I thought you were joking."

"I'm serious. Even now there are men who bury their fortune and die, and no one knows about it."

"Let's see if we can find us a buried treasure," the Englishman replied sarcastically, and chuckled.

"Don't mock me, Broker. The other day, they found a boot filled with silver by the Ledesma Lagoon, buried just a foot under the ground."

"You can never tell what goes on in a man's head," the Englishman said.

Edels didn't say anything and paced impatiently. Eli and I sat down on a log. I gazed at the moon and imagined that God was up there. Eli asked me, "Mora, is it true the world's going to end?"

"I don't know," I answered. We sat there listening to the croaking of the frogs and toads.

Then Eli told his father he had to pee, and the old man went with him. Mister Broker was leaning against the bumper of the truck, smoking, and he said to me, with his cigarette hanging from his mouth, "You like Eli, don't you?"

I didn't respond.

"You don't mind if I say that, do you? . . . Isn't it true?"

I tried to think about something else.

"Do you have a boyfriend?"

"No, sir," I replied, and looked the other way.

He walked over and put his hands on my neck. They weren't rough. I don't know why I remembered my grandfather, the way he used to hold me whenever I was afraid. Then the Englishman faced me and pointed his index finger at me, and as if he were drawing on my body, traced me from top to bottom, completely, slowly, until his finger came to rest on my belly button. His eyes focused on it, and I looked him in the face again, and saw his twisted mouth.

"We're back," Eli said at that moment.

"I want to go home," I said, and Eli said he wanted to go back too.

"Children get impatient quickly, don't they, Bruno?"

"Yes, they do."

"I'm losing my patience as well," added the Englishman, and he called his dog, and they disappeared down the road.

After a while, we heard the roaring motor of an approaching car. I recognized the jeep from the ranch and was happy to see my father. He hooked the truck to the jeep. We waited a long time, but the Englishman didn't return, and we were tired.

Bruno Edels yelled, "Where in the hell did Mister Broker go?"

My father said we'd better go look for him. It was exhausting to trudge through the rushes and mud in the pitch dark. We crossed the field and went in the direction he'd gone. We heard the sound of our boots splashing in the water.

After walking for a while, we found him, high atop a cashew tree, swearing, surrounded by wild boars grunting and banging their snouts against the trunk. My father and Edels shot at the wild pigs and they ran away. The Englishman climbed down from the tree, furious, and said that he'd wounded a boar, and that Herb had been torn to bits by those beasts.

"Have a drink, Broker," said Edels, passing him his flask.

The Englishman finished off the rest of the rum, and after calming down, muttered, "When I was in the marines it was more dangerous . . ."

"Where?"

"In Africa."

"What were you doing there?"

"We had to shoot blindly at those beasts all the time, in the middle of the jungle. I was very young."

The Englishman paused. "Come on, let's go now."

I looked at his reddish hair, his thick eyebrows, and for a moment I thought I was looking at one of those wild boar heads he'd kept as a trophy.

When we got to the truck, Mister Broker said to me, "Mora, sit up front."

"No, sir, I'm going with my father and Eli in the jeep," I said.

We left the marsh behind, and after a while, turned onto the main road. I leaned against my father's arm. Eli started to imitate the Englishman, as if it were nothing. I wanted to tell him to shut up, but didn't say anything. Then I fell asleep.

When I opened my eyes, I saw the row of eucalyptus trees, and smelled the sweet scent of the river, and realized we were entering La Lucera.

VIII

It was the Day of the Virgin. I put on my organza dress, left the house, and walked to the bus stop. While I waited, I saw the Englishman pull his jeep over to the side of the road. He asked me where I was going, and I told him, "To mass." He smiled and offered me a ride. I hesitated, but thought, after all, I didn't dislike him, and got in.

"It's an honor to give a ride to a beautiful girl," he said, laughing. "How old did you say you were, Mora?"

"I'm going to be thirteen, sir."

Stagnant water lay in the ditches. We saw a man by the barbed-wire fence, pulling a horse with a lasso. The Englishman slammed on the brakes. He grabbed his shotgun, leaned it over the lowered window of the jeep, and took aim.

"Let go of that horse, or I'll shoot you," he shouted at him.

The man seemed to take his time. The Englishman shouted at him again to hurry up, that he'd better let go of that horse that wasn't his, or he'd put a bullet in him.

The man turned the animal loose, got into his truck, and sped away. The Englishman put away his shotgun. The back of his shirt was wet and he was breathing heavily. Sweat ran down his face, and he exuded a sweet, alcoholic smell.

"Do you feel all right, sir?"

"What's that, Mora?"

"I asked you, sir, if you feel all right."

"Oh, yes. . . ."

His anger began to fade, and he leaned over me.

"Don't be frightened, child, there's a locust in your hair."
The air was heavy.

He started up the jeep, and we headed down the road again. He put a cigar in his mouth, and told her that his father had once given him a pony. The Englishman smiled; he was nice when he smiled.

"I have a book with pictures of horses. Would you like to see it?"

"Yes, sir."

"Fine, I'll show it to you soon."

A boar's tooth, hanging from the rearview mirror, swung with each pothole in the road. The Englishman took it down, and as he placed it around my neck, he said, "It's for good luck, Mora."

Suddenly, he put his hand on mine.

"Are you cold?"

"No, sir."

I felt the warmth of his hand, but I was chilled to the bone.

We reached the coast, crossed the bridge over the river, and came to the main square. I opened the door to get out, but he held me back; his hand slid between my legs, and I closed my eyes.

IX

The girl rides toward the east until she gets to the river, then stops near the dock. The Uruguay glides by like a dark brown stain. She dismounts, walks between the sandy banks to the dock, and crosses the gangplank. The Englishman is waiting for her on deck. Mora walks toward him, and he says he is happy to see her. The girl enters the galley, and the Englishman closes the door and locks it.

She looks at the things around her: a logbook, a compass, and sailor knots displayed in a frame. She wants to ask what each thing is, but is afraid to be a nuisance. She barely dares walk on the yacht, whose floor creaks with each step she takes.

The Englishman walks over, smelling of whiskey, and asks, "Where's Jordán?" It seems strange to the girl that he asks her that question.

"He left for Corrientes to bring back the herd."

The Englishman touches her braid, caresses her neck, and whispers, "I haven't seen him for a while. . . ."

Mora stands still. She does not understand why the Englishman asks about her father; after all, he was the one who sent him to drive the herd back from Pago Largo. Her heart beats wildly. The Englishman steps back.

"Does anyone know you're here, child?"

"No, sir, I did what you told me."

"Are you sure?"

"I'm sure, sir."

Silence. In the last few days, she has done nothing but think of him.

"How do you like my boat?"

"I like it very much."

The Englishman looks through the porthole, and then invites her to sit down.

"I'll get the horse book."

Mora follows him with her eyes. He stops at the bar, and she sees him light a cigar. He asks if she minds the smell, and serves himself a shot of whiskey.

Mora looks at a tin box with the British flag and a train painted on the lid, and he tells her, "It's yours."

She reads, "N° 5593 'Kolhapur.' Made in England."

Then the Englishman returns with the horse book and sits down next to her and begins to turn the pages. The girl looks at the pictures and asks whose photo is on the inside cover. He says it is his father. Drops of sweat fall from his forehead, and Mora thinks they are bubbles of whiskey bursting through his skin.

"*Caballito Blanco*, child?"

"I don't care for any, sir."

He insists that she take a sip, but again she shakes her head no, and then he opens her mouth and tips the glass, telling her, "Swallow it, baby, learn how to swallow."

Mora chokes and coughs.

He takes out his handkerchief and dries the tears sliding down her face. Then the girl begins to laugh. He laughs as well and puts his arms around her waist.

He whispers, "Mora, moramor, love me, more . . . ah . . ."

His fingers slip under her blouse, and she shudders and gets up.

"C'mon, girl! . . . Don't shy away! Where are you going?"

She looks down, her face on fire.

"You have freckles on your nose. . . ."

The Englishman laces his fingers between hers, and says he is happy to have her there. Mora lifts her head slowly and smiles.

He gives her a lingering kiss, then begins to take off her blouse, and says that nothing bad is going to happen to her. He carries her to the cabin and lays her down, whispering, "Don't be afraid, baby. . . ."

X

Summer is on its way. It has been raining for days on end. Five months have passed since that afternoon Mora was with the Englishman on his yacht. Afterward, they met many times.

One Sunday Mora arrives late for their rendezvous. She is pale, and does not look at him.

The Englishman asks her, "Why are you so late, bitch?"

She looks up, but does not answer.

"So you don't want to tell me why? Who else are you fooling around with, tell me, you little hussy," he screams at her.

"Nobody."

"Tell me the truth! Tell me who else you're screwing."

He stares at her with contempt. Mora looks with an air of helplessness at that furious man, who screams, "You think I'm going to believe you, you little whore?"

She is not afraid. He looks old to her in that brief instant when he raises his head . . . his forehead, his mouth, his eyes, much older. . . . There is something predictable about him.

"You're all a bunch of whores here," the Englishman says.

And he screams at her not to come around anymore, that he does not want to see her again. She looks at him once more and sees his twisted mouth, and remembers their first encounter that afternoon when those scraps of meat went floating by in the river.

Aunt Luisa is in the kitchen chopping onions. The girl wants to talk, to tell her what is happening, but she is afraid of how her aunt will react, and simply asks if she needs help. Aunt Luisa tells her to set the plates. Suddenly, everything blurs and darkens, and Mora collapses to the floor in a faint.

Mora opens her eyes. Aunt Luisa is kneeling at her side, fanning her. She has unfastened her dress and loosened the sash that the girl uses to cinch her bulging belly. Her aunt has a somber, impatient expression on her face. "Let me help you."

"I can manage myself."

The girl gets up slowly, adjusts the sash, and fastens her dress.

Aunt Luisa asks her, "Why are you wearing that?"

Mora does not answer, and lowers her head.

"Why, Mora?"

"For nothing, Aunt Luisa."

"Oh, my child! Do you think I don't know?"

The girl starts to cry.

"Tell me. Tell me how this happened, who was the son of a bitch? . . . Why didn't you say anything?"

Mora, between sobs, tells her it was Edels, the patrón, who raped her.

"He did it?"

The girl says yes.

"That fucking Jew. . . . Now I know why you told me that old man was a son of a bitch."

Mora dries her tears with the cuff of her dress, and tells her that she was afraid, that the old man had forbidden her to say a word.

"Please, Auntie, don't say anything to my father."

"Oh, no, Mora. We can't hide something like this from him."

"I'm very afraid, Aunt Luisa. What's going to happen when he finds out?"

"Don't worry. Leave it to me. Now, run along, change your clothes, and come back. Meanwhile, I'll finish chopping the onions."

XI ───────────────

Days later, Bruno Edels welcomes some gentlemen from the railroad company to La Lucera. After lunch, the old man and Eli show the guests around the ranch.

Mora is peeling oranges. Aunt Luisa looks at the clock and tells her, "Take the tea to the living room."

The girl obeys. Before knocking on the door, she sets the silver tray down on a little table, and hears Elsa Kessler say to the Englishman, "What you're going to give Jordán is a lot."

"My God, woman, don't ruin everything over a few pesos! We already made a deal."

"But what if Jordán changes his mind?"

"He's not going to. He's never seen so much money at one time in his life. . . ."

"But if . . ."

"Enough buts, Elsa. We pressured the old man, and he refused to give it up willingly. We have to take it from him. Jordán's the man for the job, so stop bitching, everything's already set."

Silence. Mora knocks.

Elsa tells her to come in, and the girl enters.

Mister Broker is seated with his legs crossed. The girl does not look at him.

"What are you waiting for? . . . Serve!" Elsa orders her. Mora serves the tea and it steams in the cup.

The Englishman tells her, "Sugar, child, two lumps." And he looks down at his hands.

The girl puts in the lumps of sugar and asks Elsa if she can be excused. She gives her permission, and says that the patrón and the guests will return at nine, that dinner should be ready by then, and that the guests are returning to Buenos Aires before midnight.

The girl leaves. She cannot breathe. She goes over to the window and sees her father approach the house and enter through the back door. The girl tries to understand what her father is doing there after he said that Mister Broker wanted him to bring back the herd from Pago Largo, and that he would not return until the next day. She goes over to the door and overhears the Englishman say, "Just as we discussed, Jordán, we'll give you the other half after this is over."

"Don't let us down, Jordán," says Elsa Kessler.

"Don't worry, this is like flipping a coin: heads or tails," Jordán assures them.

Everything slows down and becomes vague and blurred for the girl. Mora asks herself, "Why are they paying my father? For what?"

She returns to the kitchen. There, Aunt Luisa tells her, "Tomorrow afternoon we're going to your grandmother's house. So go on and get everything together."

The girl appears in the doorway. Then she walks to the riverbank. The water flows like a sheet of glass in the intense heat of the afternoon.

Mora hears someone singing. A tingling sensation ripples and converges in the secret recesses of her body.

Lightning. The smell of wet dirt. White crests on the river.

XII

May 24, 1932

Eli looks at the girl, bewildered, his nose pressed against the window pane of his house, as she passes by in the surrey with Aunt Luisa at her side, her head raised high. Mora pulls her dress over her knees with one hand, and with the other, grips the parasol that shades her from the afternoon sun.

Eli wonders where Mora is going with her aunt and that trunk, and he gazes at the dust the surrey leaves in its wake, and then watches as it disappears down the road.

THE AUTHOR

Perla Suez was born in Córdoba, Argentina, but lived the first fifteen years of her life in Basavilbaso, in the province of Entre Ríos, a crucial period that informs her narrative fiction, especially the three novels of *The Entre Ríos Trilogy*. Suez received a university degree in literature from the Universidad Nacional de Córdoba, Argentina, and was awarded fellowships from the French government, which enabled her to work and study from 1976-1978, at the Centro Internacional de Estudios Pedagógicos de Sèvres, during the first years of the dictatorship (1976-1983). She began her literary career publishing novels and short stories for children, and was the founding director of CEDILIJ (Centro de Difusión e Investigación de Literatura Infantil y Juvenil), a center for children's literature in Córdoba. Her novel *Memorias de Vladimir* (Alfaguara, 1992) was awarded the White Ravens Prize and has been published in several subsequent editions, most recently in 2019 by the Editorial Comunicarte. In 2000, she made her debut in the realm of adult fiction with the publication of *Letargo*, which was a finalist for the prestigious 2001 Rómulo Gallegos Prize. Since then, her popular award-winning children's novels and books have appeared in new editions, and her novels for adults have been published in translations and new editions. Her first three novels written for adults (*Letargo*, *El arresto*, and *Complot*) were published individually, and in 2006, combined into one volume entitled *Trilogía de Entre Ríos* (Editorial Norma), to coincide with the publication of the English translation, *The Entre Ríos Trilogy: Three Novels* (U of New Mexico Press). In 2008, *Trilogía de Entre Ríos* was awarded the Primer Premio Internacional Grinzane Covour. Subsequently, the Editorial Edhasa has released new editions of all three novels of the trilogy. In 2007, Suez won a Guggenheim Fellowship for her novel *La pasajera* (Editorial Norma, 2008), which was translated to English as *Dreaming of the Delta*. In 2013, she received the Argentine National Novel Prize for *Humo rojo* (Editorial Edhasa, 2012). In 2015, her novel *El país del diablo* received the Sor Juana Inés de la Cruz Literature Prize, and in 2020, the XX Rómulo Gallegos

International Novel Prize for the best novel written in Spanish in Latin America and Spain. In 2019, White Pine Press published the translation of the novel as *The Devil's Country.* In 2019, Suez published the novel *Furia de invierno* (Editorial Edhasa) to much critical acclaim, and also *Aconcagua* (Editorial Ojoreja), a book of short stories that won the 2018 Concurso de Proyectos Editoriales del Fondo de las Artes. Her works have been translated to English, French, Greek, Italian, Macedonian, Portuguese, and Serbian.

THE TRANSLATOR

Rhonda Dahl Buchanan is a Distinguished Teaching Professor of Spanish and Director of Latin American and Latino Studies at the University of Louisville. She is also the recipient of the University of Louisville Distinguished Professor Award for Outstanding Scholarship, Research, and Creative Activity. She is the author of numerous articles on contemporary Latin American writers and the editor of a book of critical essays, *El río de los sueños: Aproximaciones críticas a la obra de Ana María Shua* (2001). Her many translations include: *The Entre Ríos Trilogy* (University of New Mexico Press, 2006; 1st ed.) and *Dreaming of the Delta* (Texas Tech University Press, 2014), four novels by Perla Suez. Her translation *Quick Fix: Sudden Fiction* by Ana María Shua (White Pine Press, 2008) is a bilingual illustrated anthology of microfictions. She is the recipient of a 2006 NEA Literature Fellowship for the translation of Alberto Ruy-Sánchez's novel *The Secret Gardens of Mogador: Voices of the Earth* (White Pine Press, 2009). In 2014, White Pine Press published her translation *Poetics of Wonder: Passage to Mogador* by Alberto Ruy-Sánchez, with support from Mexico's PRO-TRAD translation program. In 2019, White Pine Press published her translation of Perla Suez's novel *The Devil's Country,* and in 2020, her translation of Mempo Giardinelli's novel *Bruno Fólner's Last Tango,* both with support from the Programa Sur Translation Support Program of the Argentine Ministry of Foreign Affairs and the University of Louisville. In 2022, her translation of Tununa Mercado's *Canon de alcoba* was published as *Chamber Canon* by Literal Publishing, with support from the Programa Sur Translation Support Program of the Argentine Ministry of Foreign Affairs and the University of Louisville.